COME AND BE KILLED and DEAR JANET ROSENBERG, DEAR MR. KOONING

This is the third volume of plays by Stanley Eveling to be published. He is undoubtedly one of the most accomplished, varied and original new British dramatists. Mr. Eveling, who teaches moral philosophy at Edinburgh University, is very concerned with moral problems and he imposes his ideas strongly on all his plays.

This is particularly so in Come and Be Killed, a powerful and darkly humorous play about the effects of an intended abortion on a previously free-and-easy relationship. Dear Janet Rosenberg, Dear Mr. Kooning deals with the poignant and funny relationship between an established author, Alec Kooning, and a devoted female admirer, Janet Rosenberg. It has wit, pathos and humour in abundance and was recently successfully produced 'off-off Broadway' in New York by Max Stafford-Clark, who also directed it in Great Britain at the Traverse Theatre Club, Edinburgh and the Theatre Upstairs at the Royal Court.

By the same author:

PLAYSCRIPT 37

'come and be killed' & 'dear janet rosenberg, dear mr kooning'

stanley eveling

CALDER AND BOYARS · LONDON

First published in Great Britain 1971
by Calder and Boyars Limited
18 Brewer Street, London W1R 4AS

ISBN   0 7145 0749 0   Cloth edition
ISBN   0 7145 0750 4   Paper edition

Printed by photo-lithography
and made in Great Britain at
The Pitman Press, Bath.

CONTENTS

COME AND BE KILLED

COME AND BE KILLED was first performed at the Traverse Theatre Club, Edinburgh, on 13th July, 1967 with the following cast:

JIM	Robert Morris
BETTINA	Francesca Annis
JERRY	Tim Seely
CHRISTINE	Annabel Leventon

The play was directed by Milo Sperber.

ACT ONE

Scene One

(The scene is the same throughout the play: a room containing the usual appurtenances of a bachelor's one room, plus a kitchen alcove which is situated S.R. S.L. there is a low, white bed and right of the bed, some chairs and a round table. Also S.L. is the door to the stairs leading to the external world. S.R. is a telephone. There should be plenty of books, bookcases, a flat-topped desk, a sideboard, a lot of paper (newspapers, that is), one or two objets trouves. A painting or two, perhaps a piece of sculpture, or the wire model for a piece of sculpture, that sort of thing. The play opens in darkness with a late bit of Beethoven's 9th playing. It plays. There is a female sigh and then a snoring sound)

BETTINA. You're asleep! (Switches off the tape recorder)

(The snoring chokes off, there is a sleepy mutter, sound of a body being shifted and then a snort and clearing of the throat. BETTINA switches on a table lamp situated on the floor beside her. She is stretched on the floor, resting her back on the side of the bed whereon is stretched JIM, flat out, mouth open. When the light is switched on, he opens and closes his mouth, opens his eyes. The GIRL gets up, stretches, looks at him)

BETTINA. What a sight!

JIM. (closes his eyes) Coffee ... !

9

BETTINA. You're an animal, d'you know that?

JIM. A cup of hot, steaming coffee.

BETTINA. You were asleep. (She moves out to the kitchen)

JIM. (opens one eye, stares after her) Yea, I heard it, though.

BETTINA. You don't give a damn about higher things.

JIM. What is a higher thing?

BETTINA. Art.

JIM. I do. I love art. I didn't like the interpretation, that's all.

(BETTINA makes a rude sound. JIM hums a few bars on the 9th)

JIM. My feeling is the tempi was all to cock.

BETTINA. What did you say?

JIM. His tempi ...

BETTINA. What about his tempi?

JIM. It was all to cock. No sensitivity: that's what's wrong with him.

(The phone rings. JIM is irritated)

JIM. The phone's ringing.

BETTINA. Yes.

JIM. Answer it, then.

BETTINA. You answer it.

JIM. I can't reach.

BETTINA. (comes in with coffee) One hot, steaming bowl.
10

JIM. Answer that phone, will you?

BETTINA. Here, my fingers are burning.

JIM. Oh, for Christ's sake. (He takes the cup)

(BETTINA picks up the phone)

Ta, angel.

BETTINA. Yes, what? What? No ... no.

(She slams the phone down`

JIM. Who was it?

BETTINA. Wrong number.

JIM. Ah! (He sips his coffee)

(BETTINA goes out to get her coffee)

You know, you shouldn't slam the phone down like that. It just damages the phone.

BETTINA. (returning) I know.

JIM. Well, you shouldn't do it, then.

BETTINA. I know. (She sits down in her former position. Takes a sip of coffee. Puts it down. Begins to straighten her stockings)

JIM. (stares, bemused) I'll tell you somcthing else.

BETTINA. What?

JIM. (still bemused) You shouldn't slam the phone down.

BETTINA. What? (She notes his famished stare; adjusts her skirt. Makes a kissing movement with her lips)

JIM. Bettina.

BETTINA. Hmmm?

JIM. Give yourself.

BETTINA. No.

JIM. Come on. Just once.

BETTINA. Come on. Just once.

BETTINA. No. I don't believe in it.

JIM. You don't have to believe in it. You just have to
enjoy it.

BETTINA. It's not right.

JIM. Why? ... It's not illegal.

BETTINA. Morally speaking ...

JIM. That is the most preposterous remark I've ever had
the misfortune to hear.

BETTINA. Possibly.

JIM. Well, just come up beside me and have a snog then.
(He bends his head over the bed, puts his face beside
hers)

BETTINA. I can't drink coffee and snog as you call it ...

JIM. Eh? (Twiddles her hair) Come on.

BETTINA. Jimmy!

JIM. (flops back. Begins to examine his feet) A snog. Just
a snog. (Meditates) Snog. Snog. It sounds as if it
consists of blowing your nose in somebody else's
handkerchief.

BETTINA. (puts her coffee down) Do you mind.

JIM. You know what Freud would say?

BETTINA. Yes.

(Pause)

JIM.   Freud would say you're keeping hold of it because you have an aggressive desire to assert yourself against me.

BETTINA.   Freud wouldn't say that.

JIM.   Well, Freud's wrong then. You know what Lawrence would say.

BETTINA.   Yes.

JIM.   Lawrence would say you were refusing to submit to the dark gods.

(Pause)

The deep, instinctual flow ... and all that.

BETTINA.   There's plenty of time for the deep instinctual flow ... and all that ... the important this is to respect each other.

JIM.   (shocked into sitting up) Have you seen my socks?

BETTINA.   Nowadays people don't respect each other.

JIM.   Respect! You must be out of your mind.

BETTINA.   It's all grab this, grab that. People should stop and think.

JIM.   I am thinking.

BETTINA.   Well?

JIM.   My present thought is "Have you seen my socks?"

BETTINA.   No. What's so special about your socks?

JIM.   Ha, ha. (Leans over. Sees his socks which she is half-sitting on) If we're going to be respectable, which is all your respect comes to, I might as well cover these

13

lewd, naked feet of mine. (He wiggles his toes in his socks) I say, Bettina, these socks _are_ warm.

BETTINA. Sexy ...

JIM. Bettina!

BETTINA. No.

JIM. (sarcastically) Don't you want it, then?

BETTINA. Possibly ... (considers) Perhaps ... Almost certainly.

JIM. Well, lovey, if you want it and I want it, let's have it. It seems the rational thing to do.

BETTINA. I respect you too much.

JIM. Listen, Bettina, don't respect me. Just regard me with unutterable contempt ... because that's what I am, contemptible ... in many ways ... Just regard me an an extremely appetising but utterly contemptible piece of meat. Just satisfy your hunger and leave it at that.

BETTINA. No, I insist on respecting you.

JIM. But I don't want to be respected. I've got no time for it. There's nothing I want less to be than respected. It's an intolerable attitude. Respect's a thing that has to be _lived up to_ ... Once you're respected, you're in a strait jacket, a strait jacket, moreover, made to some other lunatic's specifications. I absolutely refuse to live _up_ to anything ... It's a deplorable way to behave.

BETTINA. I respect you, I tell you. There's nothing you can do about it.

JIM. Take you and that bloody classical music ...

BETTINA. It was beautiful.

JIM. What's that got to do with it?

BETTINA. What?

JIM. Well, you think because it's classical crap you have to listen to it with a kind of awful reverence. It's disgusting; it's like atheists tip-toeing about in church.

BETTINA. I like it.

JIM. I've never been respected in the whole of my life. I never thought to see the day when I would live to be respected. I've always seen the signs of it before.

BETTINA. You think anything that takes time and trouble to enjoy is a load of old rubbish ...

JIM. As soon as I've seen the signs of it, I've always managed to do something that stopped it dead in its tracks.

BETTINA. Respect is finding out what's to be admired in something or someone and then admiring it.

JIM. Jesus, that's terrible.

BETTINA. You're a fine man.

JIM. No, no. Listen, Bettina, and I'll tell you a cautionary nightmare I had once.

BETTINA. You have qualities ...

JIM. In this nightmare, love, I was walking along this avenue ... and on the avenue there was a notice and on the notice it said "This way to respect". Now when I saw that notice I was pussy-struck. (Meditatively) The trees were those tall, thin ones ...

BETTINA. Poplars. Very Freudian.

JIM. Yes, well, that's an irrelevance. I stopped ... or rather I tried to stop but me legs would keep going.

Bloody legs, I shouted, bloody silly legs, you're
going the wrong way. But on and on they went.

BETTINA. Hmmm.

JIM. The next notice said "Doff your hat, you're meeting
with respect ..." And sure enough, just ahead there
was this bloody dais and on it, Bettina, you'll never
believe this, there was this bloody great big English
sheep dog. A great big fat stupid friendly-looking
dog with hair in its eyes. I thought "I'll boot it up
the arse. That'll show respect."

BETTINA. What happened then, you liar?

JIM. It lifted up its leg and peed all over my trousers.

BETTINA. It's no good. You can't evade my remorseless
respect.

JIM. But what's the point of it? What I mean is, it's a
bloody impertinent emotion. It's an intrusion of the
outside on the inside. What you should do, Bettina, is
to reserve your respect for public figures; Royalty,
Archbishops, those whom God has called to high
office and that ... do you not understand?

BETTINA. If I didn't respect you, I couldn't respect
myself.

JIM. (giving up) I don't respect myself. I enjoy myself.
That is what I consider I was given myself to do ...
with ... (To himself) Speaking personally, I blame
modern education.

BETTINA. James ...

JIM. What?

BETTINA. Supposing we did make love ...

JIM. Supposing intimacy did occur ... yes?

BETTINA. Either we'd have a baby, or we wouldn't.

16

JIM. (bending over. Attempts to kiss her ear, etc; she is
     indifferent) Either you'd have a baby or you wouldn't
     ... very true ... indisputable.

BETTINA. Now. Supposing we did ...

JIM. What a fine young baba it would be ...

BETTINA. Ah, but what would happen to it?

JIM. It would get its snotty little gob rubbed in it like
     everybody else.

BETTINA. And what would happen to me?

JIM. You'd be its mum-mum.

BETTINA. And you'd be its dad-dad.

JIM. (uncomfortably) What about the other limb of the
     hypothesis?

BETTINA. Ah, now, if I didn't ... then one day you'd see
     some other bright young bird and you'd know no peace
     till you'd lured it in here and feathered your nest...

JIM. As it were.

BETTINA. There you are, then.

JIM. (sits back) Ah!

BETTINA. You've seen the light.

JIM. Aha.

BETTINA. Good.

JIM. Aha, aha. (Rises from the bed)

BETTINA. Haven't you, Jimmy?

JIM. There is a flaw in your argument.

BETTINA. Nonsense.

JIM. There is a great big sham-bollicle flaw in your deduction ...

BETTINA. I was unaware ...

JIM. ... a great hole in your dialectical bucket, dear Liza ... a hole ...

BETTINA. (flatly. A genuine question) Do you love me?

JIM. A dirty big crack, right in the foundations.

BETTINA. (flatly) Do you love me?

JIM. Because what I say is ... I knew you'd get round to that question ... What I say is it doesn't follow from the fact that you respect me that you don't have to sleep with me, as the euphemism has it; otherwise all the sleeping partners there's ever been, out of wedlock that is, wouldn't have respected each other ... witness ...

BETTINA. Well, do you?

JIM. Tristan and Isolde. She respected him alright. Daphnis and Chloe ... there was a lot of respect in that relationship ... and (triumphantly) Heloise and Abelard ... now, she was a nun and he lost every - thing ... so you can't say there wasn't dignity and respect and person-hood in that situation. I think I may be said to have cut the ground from under your position, Bettina.

BETTINA. Answer my question.

JIM. We've only known each other a month.

BETTINA. Not too soon for you to want a degree of physical intimacy beyond such a meagre acquaintance-ship.

JIM. Well?

BETTINA. But not long enough to mean anything else, apparently.

JIM. As you well know, physical relationships don't need time to mature. They spring up in the darkness and die at the dawn of light. I mean, I've only known this coffee for about five minutes, but I'm not going to wait until our relationship ripens into something deeper before I drink it.

BETTINA. Women are different.

JIM AND BETTINA. Viva la difference! (They become more relaxed)

JIM. Women always ask you that, you know ... "Do you love me?" It's pathetic ... ! "Do you love me?"

BETTINA. Well, why not? They want to be valued. They want to hear an expression of feeling for them. Women definitely do not like to be regarded as a something to satisfy an appetite.

JIM. "I love you" is never an expression of feeling. It's a declaration of intent.

BETTINA. (gets up. Goes to the mirror) I don't think I'm going to sleep with a man till I'm married ... (She admires herself) It wouldn't be fair to him.

JIM. Which?

BETTINA. Either.

JIM. I don't mind.

BETTINA. Good.

JIM. Sleep with me.

BETTINA. No.

JIM. Sleep with me, Bettina. I worship you.

BETTINA. Liar.

JIM. I love you.

BETTINA. You're not serious about anything.

JIM. I'm not a hypocrite.

BETTINA. You are if you say you love me.

JIM. Ah, but I didn't mean it.

BETTINA. That's what being a hypocrite is!

JIM. Is it? I never know.

BETTINA. Hopeless. (Moves over to the desk where there are nine volumes of an encyclopaedia) Jimmy, why have you got only nine volumes of this encyclopaedia?

JIM. I told you. I'm only responsible for A to I. From A to I I'm an extremely enlightened person. It all goes a bit dark after that.

BETTINA. (takes up a volume, weighs it admiringly) Still, A to I's a lot; they're very heavy.

JIM. It's not the weight I object to, it's the content.

BETTINA. Well, I think editing an encyclopaedia must be very interesting.

JIM. It's horrible. As far as I can see from the stuff they send in most of the contributors are illiterate and all of them type with their thumbs.

BETTINA. (opens a volume. Looks in it) Do you know, Jimmy, in the short time I've known you I've never actually seen you doing any work. You seem to spend most of your time talking or lying on that bed with your eyes closed.

JIM. Ah, you mustn't be taken in by superficial appearances, Bettina. I have the sort of brain that operates best in a recumbent posture. When I'm lying here with me eyes shut and me mouth open, I seem to be sleeping, don't I?

BETTINA. Yes you do.

JIM. Well, I'm not. All the time me great brain is grinding its way to the bottom of things ...

BETTINA. So when other people are doing what they call sleeping you're doing what you call working ...

JIM. Exactly. One day there'll be a click! I'll rise from me bed reeling with knowledge ... instead of wasting me wonderful brains on the mouldering gobbets of geriatric scholars. That'll be the day I use that disgusting encyclopaedia for its true purpose, page by rotten page. Ugh. Do you know, Bettina, I once nearly didn't get an article on Gypsies because the drunken tinker they got to write it thought you spelled it with a J.

BETTINA. (reading) It says here that the Ichnsuman fly ...

JIM. (unctuously) An hymonopterous insect abounding in many lands.

BETTINA. It says it knows exactly the right spot at which to strike its caterpillar victim in order to render it helpless.

JIM. Yes. I learned a lot from that fly ... (gets up, comes towards BETTINA, puts his arms around her)

BETTINA. Ugh, it says here ...

JIM. (whispers) Let me tell you about Ephemoptera.

BETTINA. It says here ... (He turns her round)

JIM. Ephemoptera, Bettina, are sorrowful little insects that exist in a larval condition for two or three years. But as soon as they arrive at maturity, and this is the sad bit, their little lives hurry to a close. They rise up, in pyramids, Bettina ...

BETTINA. Fancy that.

JIM. In pyramids, Bettina, on warm summer nights. They rise up, take no food, propagate, and then die.

BETTINA. Do they? (They look at each other)

JIM. Yes, they do.

(She turns back to her book)

BETTINA. It says here ...

(He nuzzles her neck, makes a buzzing sound)

What're you doing?

JIM. I'm striking you in the right spot in order to render you helpless. (He kisses her neck. She remains obdurate and cold. He stands back. Stares at her) So much for the rotten abounding Ichnsuman fly. I could always rape you of course.

BETTINA. I doubt it.

JIM. I could, I could. I've read about it. The Heath murders.

BETTINA. Ugh!

JIM. In the H's. He ...

BETTINA. Shut up ...

JIM. He tied their legs and arms to the bed-posts, and had them solid till he was a physical wreck and then chopped them into messes. Dr. Yellowlees, the psychiatrist, said that Heath did not know the difference between right and wrong.

BETTINA. Poor man. What happened to him?

JIM. Yellowlees...he's still...

BETTINA. Heath!

JIM. They hanged him, the bastard. Heath, that is.

BETTINA. I thought you didn't believe in capital punishment.

JIM. I don't believe in it. But I feel very strongly that bastards like that should be hung, drawn and quartered. It makes me very uneasy.

BETTINA. Well, I'm glad they stopped all that, anyway.

JIM. Yes. It's a good thing. I have all the right beliefs, you know ... Yanks go home, ban the bomb, down with Polaris, coloured people ... but my feelings reveal themselves as definitely on the side of the brute.

BETTINA. You've got a split personality.

JIM. Yes ... a schizophrenic conscience ... Why don't you ... (He moves towards her)

BETTINA. I think I'd better go.

JIM. (irritated) I don't know why you came.

BETTINA. Don't you?

JIM. No, I don't ...

BETTINA. I like you. I had hopes.

JIM. So did I, by God.

BETTINA. I thought we might be able to ...

JIM. I'm able but you're not willing ...

BETTINA. Why is it that whenever I try to be serious, you try to make me sound pretentious?

JIM. You should ponder that fact.

BETTINA. Perhaps I should.

JIM. Bettina ... you're really the nicest, most interesting and pleasantest girl person I've met for some weeks. But these things apart I am appealing to you, in all honesty, and purely at the level of animal interest ... will you?

(BETTINA sighs)

JIM. It could be so pleasant. Once we're over the hump.

BETTINA. (bites her nails, says with eyes big, ironic) The hump?

JIM. Yes. (Stares at her)

BETTINA. (brusquely) Alright.

JIM. Eh?

BETTINA. Alright ... what do I do? (Helplessly)

JIM. How d'you mean? It's perfectly straightforward ... we ... er ...

BETTINA. I don't mean that.

JIM. Well, for one thing, one behaves with a little more subtlety, a little more finesse; one sort of lets it happen, one's will is, so to speak, slowly drugged and seduced... ; a sort of drowsy tide of lust; one ... er ... oh, get into bed and further instructions will follow.

BETTINA. Put the light off.

JIM. (switches the light off) Thank God for some decency anyway.

24

BETTINA. Decency. Respect, you mean.

JIM. Respect ... Bettina ... Bettina ... I respect you ...
I respect your toes and your knees and the warm part
of your mouth and your buttocks and your lovely
warm back and your beautiful ... that's what I respect, Bettina.

BETTINA. I don't think I'm going to enjoy this.

JIM. Consciousness, my angel, is the enemy of desire ...

Scene Two

(Darkness again. Weeks later. Perhaps the flat has
a slightly more domesticated appearance. On the bookcase a big china cock)

BETTINA. Jimmy ... Jimmy ...

JIM. Ugh ... What time is it?

BETTINA. It moved.

(Pause)

JIM. What's the time?

BETTINA. Did you not hear what I said? It moved.

JIM. Well, what's o'clock (A passable imitation of Olivier
in Richard III)

BETTINA. (switches light on, leaning over him to do
it. Takes his or her wristwatch and stares at it)
God, it's nearly half-past nine.

JIM. It's the middle of the bloody night. Would you like
some coffee?

BETTINA. (absent-mindedly) Yes, please.

JIM. It shouldn't take you a minute.

BETTINA. I'm sure I felt it move.

JIM. Well, you're not sending it to get the coffee, are you?

BETTINA. What?

JIM. I was joking.

BETTINA. What?

JIM. (getting up) Nothing. (Goes out. BETTINA touches her stomach. Is inwardly concentrated) Where's the bloody kettle? Ouch!

BETTINA. What's the matter?

JIM. I've cut my foot.

BETTINA. What?

JIM. Nothing. It's nothing serious. Just a small slash running from my toe to the back of my foot.

BETTINA. The kettle's on the side.

JIM. (very irritated) Which side?... (pause) Side of what?

BETTINA. (resigned) Hang on.

JIM. (now he has won the point) It's alright. (Sound of pouring water) It couldn't've moved.

BETTINA. I felt it.

JIM. No, you didn't. (Comes back in) It's only eight weeks. It's just a little raw, red, wrinkled, inscrutable organism at the moment.

BETTINA. If it's moving, I'm not having it done.

JIM. Yes, it's just huffing and puffing it's way up the

evolutionary ladder at the moment. It's got through the tails and fins stage and now it's trying to creep up on land.

BETTINA. (refuses to be put off) I'm not, Jimmy.

JIM. Go and make the coffee.

BETTINA. Yes, sir.

(He catches hold of her)

(She fingers the hair of his chest) What do you desire, your furryness?

JIM. You shouldn't wrinkle your forehead like that.

BETTINA. Ah, you're protecting my beauty, darling.

JIM. It's the only thing you've got.

BETTINA. Ta, very much.

JIM. (he hunches up his shoulders) Do I look like something?

BETTINA. No.

JIM. What do I look like?

BETTINA. Er ...

JIM. You'll never guess. I'm an Ecballium.

BETTINA. An Ec what?

JIM. An Ecballium. Known in more refined circles as the Squirting Cucumber.

BETTINA. I don't believe you.

JIM. It's a fact. It is so named because when it is ripe it breaks from the stalk and ejects its seeds and juice from the aperture made by the breakage.

BETTINA. What a revolting vegetable thing!

JIM. Pricpic, that's what I am. A martyr to continuous erections. It's no joke.

BETTINA. Go and make the coffee.

JIM. Mmmm. (Goes out) I'm sick of making coffee. The years are marked out in bottles of Maxwell House. The number of bottles is all recorded in the book of the great Grocer himself. "Ah", says he, "he's on to his last bottle now". And I won't know ... one day they'll come in and find me stretched out, struck down by the last colossal blow, and standing pathetically there, symbol of life, in all its idiotic, mystic variety, will be a half-used bottle of Maxwell House ... which they will take away with them.

BETTINA. (laying the table for breakfast) Swingin'.

JIM. (poking his head round the door) Do you ever imagine your end?

BETTINA. Sometimes.

(His head goes back again)

Not like you, though. (To herself)

JIM. What?

BETTINA. Not like you ...

JIM. Ah?

BETTINA. More humdrum ... less dramatic ... my end will be. Surrounded by my heavy-eyed children ... I can't really imagine it. And neither can you.

JIM. (comes in with coffee) Oh, mine won't be heroic. A scruffy, nasty, old man in bedsocks, all yellow with pee ... No ... I lie ... on second thoughts ... (He fumbles for a cigarette)

BETTINA. Don't smoke before breakfast ...

JIM. (Ignores her) I'll probably go early. (He offers her a cigarette)

(She takes it. They light up)

Surrounded by young doctors and giggling, solemn, aseptic ... Catholic ... nurses ... with sterilised pudenda... (Between "aseptic" and "Catholic" and "nurses" and with etc", he has taken huge gulps of smoke) who will insist upon trying to cheer me up. The bastards.

BETTINA. (smokes) How do you know it couldn't've moved?

JIM. It's too early.

BETTINA. Suppose it had.

JIM. (at an anxious loss) Well ... well ... what do you want to suppose that for?

BETTINA. Because I'm not having it done if it moved and that's flat.

JIM. No.

BETTINA. You don't seem very certain.

JIM. Oh ... I am ... I am. (Begins to butter some bread. They can fiddle with Cornflakes, etc., throughout the scene) It's just it's a funny distinction, that's all.

BETTINA. When it's moved it's ...

JIM. (begins to munch a piece of toast) The Catholics think they can tell when the soul gets itself inserted into the body. After that it's murder.

BETTINA. Don't.

JIM. Sorry.

BETTINA. Do you think ...

JIM. No ... I've thought already.

BETTINA. You don't know what I'm going to say ...

JIM. I do. We've made up our minds.

BETTINA. It's just I don't know what we've made up our minds for.

JIM. (wryly) We're not married.

BETTINA. Well ... !

JIM. For Christ's sake. You're ruining my breakfast ... and my foot's hurting ... it's hurting terribly. (Rolls down his sock) This leg is turning green!

BETTINA. You don't bloody care, do you?

JIM. Cabbage green. God almighty ... (bangs his foot) Turn pink, will you!

BETTINA. Do you?

JIM. No ... I don't ... not in that way ...

BETTINA. What way?

(He munches another piece of toast)

What way?

JIM. Any way ...

BETTINA. What? ... (Gloomily) I wish I didn't have any choice.

JIM. Ah, well, there you have a point. (Groans) Oh ... I'm definitely damaged.

BETTINA. Jim.

JIM. Mmmm?

BETTINA. Why don't we get married?

JIM. I've told you. I'm not ready for that sort of thing yet. I'm too young.

BETTINA. You're 28 ... aren't you?

JIM. What's my chronological age got to do with it?

BETTINA. What do you mean you're not ready for it, then?

JIM. There are larger things in life.

BETTINA. What larger things? You hate your work, you hardly move from your bed ... !

JIM. I'm in a state of preparation ... !

BETTINA. But what for?

JIM. I don't know ... I feel it ... like a chrysalis ... it doesn't know what beautiful thing it's going to turn into but it's preparing itself all the time ... when it comes ... the call ... I'll be here, ready.

BETTINA. So that's what you're waiting for ... to change into a beautiful thing!

JIM. Metaphorically speaking, yes ...

BETTINA. That's stupid. People acquire obligations. It's quite different for people.

JIM. Lies. Bloody propaganda. I've told you once and I've told you twice and this is the last time ... I do not want this baby and I do not want this marriage, and even if I did, I wouldn't have either ... (Dumb pause) ... because ...

BETTINA. Alright ... I get the message ...

31

JIM. It's not ... it's just ... because if we have it ... if we get married ... if we do ... well, that's it ... bloody well all arranged, me, you, it, babies, houses, all wrapped up, finished, all tied up ready for the insurance agent, the bloody undertaker ... they'll be queuing outside the door ... I can't explain ... it's because it's so absolutely and completely certain and flat and ordinary and known and arranged ... I don't know ... I have inclinations elsewhere ... other failures to organise ... outside all that ... this ... I will not be dictated to by a biological mechanism. That's what it comes down to ... I have a choice and I have chosen. Okay?

(During these remarks BETTINA elaborately butters herself some toast and eats it, not looking at anything)

BETTINA. Right.

JIM. Right.

BETTINA. Right.

JIM. I have a more grandiose idea ... I can't describe it ...

BETTINA. Right.

JIM. Uuuuuuugh ... It's bloody squalid. Your bloody insides are squalid ... !

BETTINA. (obdurately) If we had it ...

JIM. (bellows) NO ... !!

BETTINA. If I had it ...

JIM. Oh, well, that's up to you ...

BETTINA. If I had it ...

JIM. Of course, I'd help ... if you wanted help ...

BETTINA. I just wonder what it would be like ...

JIM. I don't know. Probably rather bright and extremely good looking, a rather sturdy but strikingly sensitive child.

BETTINA. Like you, you mean.

JIM. Possibly ...

BETTINA. I wonder what I'd call it ...

JIM. Jemima ...

BETTINA. That's rather a nice name. Jemima. Or if it was a boy I'd call it by some Anglo-Saxon name ... Richard ... or something like that ...

JIM. That's not an Anglo-Saxon name. There's absolutely nothing Anglo-Saxon about that. Anglo-Saxons had names like Aethelbert or Ragwort or Aelfstan ...

BETTINA. Aelfstan ...

JIM. Yes ... what's the matter?

BETTINA. I don't know ... it's just that giving it a name makes a difference somehow ... it gives it an identity ...

(Pause)

JIM. Does it ... ? Would you like some more coffee?

BETTINA. No ... yes, yes I would ...

(JIM goes out to put the kettle on)

JIM. Strictly speaking, that's not true ...

BETTINA. What isn't ... ?

JIM. That bit about giving it an identity. Strictly speaking ... (He pours in the water) an organism, a human organism, that is, gets identity when it comes to consciousness. Strictly speaking ...

BETTINA. It'd be wrong to have it done if it's moved. That
means it's alive. (She takes a cigarette)

JIM. Alive? (Comes to the door) What difference does
that make?

BETTINA. You'd soon find out if you were dead.

JIM. It's coming to consciousness that makes the difference.

BETTINA. Before it moves it's not alive, so it's not wrong,
then. At least ...

JIM. "Alive" is just a word. (Comes further into the
room) It's "alive" before that ... it's living ...

BETTINA. Is it?

JIM. No you don't.

BETTINA. If it's alright to kill it before it's alive ...

JIM. Before it's alive you can't ... ugh ... (Returns to
the kitchen)

BETTINA. (raising her voice) Why is it wrong to kill it
after it's alive?

JIM. (begins making coffee) I don't know. All I know is
it'd be wrong if it was aware of what's going on.

JIM. Yes they are.

BETTINA. Well what about before they're born then ... ?

(She goes into the kitchen)

JIM. Well, possibly I was wrong. I'm not an expert on
pre-natal and post-natal awareness. Sugar?

BETTINA. Here ... (She takes the sugar. Begins to spoon
it in)

JIM. Perhaps it's when they can feel pain ...

BETTINA. What?

JIM. Look out what you're doing ...

BETTINA. Perhaps it feels pain before it's born though ...

JIM. Impossible ... where's the milk ... ?

BETTINA. How do you know?

(They come back in, carrying cups)

JIM. This is all abstract speculation. Before it's alive ...
(Looks for milk) It's not here ...

BETTINA. That's only a word ...

JIM. All I can say is ... (Looking around)

BETTINA. It's next door ...

JIM. Eh?

BETTINA. If you're looking for the milk ...

JIM. Oh ... (Moves towards door) It wasn't in the plan ...

BETTINA. (following him) No, it wasn't in the plan.

JIM. If it wasn't included in the plan, it wasn't included ...
that much is obvious ... Listen, Bo-Peep, it's no
use following me around ... you don't take milk ...

(She continues to put milk in her coffee)

BETTINA. Circumstances alter cases ...

JIM. You don't take milk ...

BETTINA. Blast ...

JIM. Not every time, they don't. It's still a matter for
decision ... (He comes through)

(BETTINA stays to make herself more coffee)

(He slumps down in a chair) We didn't start out with the idea of fornicating for procreation, did we?

BETTINA. But that's what happened.

JIM. It didn't ... all that's happened is a couple of cells have joined forces and if left to themselves and all the little bits and pieces inside (bitterly) you, ultimately, a small creature'll plop out ... emerge ... (stares moodily ahead) ... plop ...

BETTINA. (comes in) What?

JIM. I said "a small creature'll plop out".

BETTINA. Yes.

JIM. No.

BETTINA. (sits down) I don't know what to do.

JIM. Well, that's up to you. I'm not deciding for you, so don't pretend I am. I've decided.

BETTINA. I know where you stand.

JIM. Right.

BETTINA. (gloomily) There's not much love around here, is there?

JIM. No.

BETTINA. I wish I was dead ...

JIM. Dilly, dilly, dilly, dilly, Come and be killed.

(He puts his arms around her)

BETTINA. Butcher.

JIM. Not I.

36

BETTINA. Please ...

JIM. Bettina! I can't give you permission. You have to make up your own mind ...

BETTINA. I can't.

JIM. You must.

BETTINA. I can't. I can't. Help me.

JIM. How can I?

BETTINA. Say you want it.

JIM. I can't say that.

BETTINA. Yes, you can. You don't have to mean it. Say to want it and afterwards ...

JIM. Afterwards I say "push off". Is that right?

BETTINA. If you want to.

JIM. (he moves away) No, no, no. It's just a piece of rotten self-deception. You're half-hoping ... The trouble is ... what're you hoping for? Before you got pregnant you didn't want a thingamajig ... right? ... now you have, you do ... it's stupid ...

BETTINA. It's just the idea ...

JIM. Well, forget it. It's nothing. An idea's a bubble in your head. Think of the facts.

BETTINA. (contemptuously) Facts!

JIM. The facts are that hundreds of people get abortions, thousands ... there's an abortion once every two minutes ...

BETTINA. That's births ...

JIM. It's just a few minutes and then it's all over ... then

37

we can decide things. It'll be up to us to decide ...

BETTINA. We're supposed to be deciding now ...

JIM. You know what I mean ... it'll clear the air ...
we won't be all muddled and mixed up and confused
... it's no good ...

BETTINA. I suppose you're right.

JIM. Of course I am.

BETTINA. Afterwards it'll be up to us. I mean, we might
grow sick of the sight of each other ...

JIM. Yes ...

BETTINA. Or we might not ...

JIM. Correct ...

BETTINA. Anyway, I've got this degree to finish ...

JIM. That's a good point.

BETTINA. And you've got this great thing that's in your
plan.

JIM. Exactly ...

BETTINA. This great thing ... !

(Pause)

That's that, then.

JIM. Great.

BETTINA. Great it is ...

(Pause)

JIM. I've got old non-swingin' sooper Jerry coming round
later ...

BETTINA. Who's Jerry ...

JIM. You've heard me speak of sooper old sooper Jerry and his sooper, marvellous, antivivisexualist, dolly chick wife, ... haven't you?

BETTINA. If she's the one you go on about, she's no dolly-chick ...

JIM. No, but she's <u>sooper</u> ...

BETTINA. What's he coming round for?

JIM. He's ... er ... well ... he knows all the people ... he's ... er ...

BETTINA. Oh!

JIM. If you'd rather leave it to me ...

BETTINA. Leave <u>what</u> to you?

JIM. Hey ... don't look so glum, eh? Get with it ... give yourself a chance, eh ... trust old Jim ... Jim, 'e knows best ... 'e does ... just you trust old Jim.

BETTINA. Somehow neither the voice nor the accent inspires confidence.

JIM. (shrugs his shoulders. Speaks his version of what he imagines a Jewish intonation would be) I should be so lucky!

BETTINA. You don't have to ...

JIM. It's a living ... you know what I mean ... (slouches towards her, like Olivier, in Richard III)..., "meantime I'll marry with the lady Anne" ...

(They look at each other)

"whom I slew in my angry mood ... at (he shrieks out) Tewkesbury".

(Pause)

No? Tewkesbury's a hole ...

BETTINA. Is it?

JIM. (brusquely) Anyway, as I was saying, Jerry's coming round so if you want to we'll fix it all up and then all you've got to do ...

BETTINA. All I've got to do is to go and get aborted.

JIM. Mmmm.

BETTINA. That's all. Uuuuugh.

JIM. I know ...

BETTINA. I hate bloody men.

JIM. What you mean is you wish you were one.

(BETTINA begins to tidy up the breakfast table)

BETTINA. I honestly believe I wish nothing of the sort. You know what I think?

JIM. (climbing back onto the bed) No, Bettina. My sock is slowly filling with blood. Then it'll congeal like red cement and that'll be that.

BETTINA. I honestly think men don't have any emotions ... They're more like mechanical things ...

JIM. Clank, clank ...

BETTINA. They have plans, schemes, appetites, even feelings ...

JIM. Crikey!

BETTINA. ... attitudes, perhaps ...

JIM. (in a shocked tone) Attitudes ... never!

40

BETTINA. ... but apart from that, they don't seem to know anything, what anything's like ... they're always

(JIM makes mad gestures with his fingers, mutters)

working things out, describing things ...

JIM. "And the <u>great</u> organ rises in the <u>great</u> temple".

BETTINA. <u>You</u>, for instance ...

JIM. (in a mechanical voice) I listen ...

BETTINA. You talk ... you know all the right words ... your syntax is usually correct, your ability to move from one sound to another

(He makes a strangled sound in his throat)

is considerable ... but that's all. You don't experience anything. You're like a dictionary with appetites.

JIM. A dictionary which, at the moment, lies open at the letter F.

BETTINA. With you, everything's a joke, everything's a word.

JIM. Is it?

BETTINA. Oh, it doesn't matter ...

JIM. Everything's a word, eh?

BETTINA. Forget it.

JIM. No, no, you're right, you're quite right. I sometimes think I'm really just a sort of verbal self-awareness; I mean, I sometimes think that all I am is a sort of unknowing thing with words bobbing about on top of it.

BETTINA. Oh, well, who isn't?

JIM. Hundreds of people ...

(Begins slowly taking off his sock. Draws in his breath)

BETTINA. Maybe.

JIM. You, for one. You're not like that.

BETTINA. Oh, me. I'm just stupid.

JIM. No you're not. What do you want to say that for? You're very clever.

BETTINA. No, I'm not.

JIM. You bloody are. One of the top five per cent ...

BETTINA. Am I?

JIM. Christ ... of course you are. That's the trouble ... Better a pig satisfied than Socrates unsatisfied ...

BETTINA. You think it'd be better if I was stupid ...

JIM. Were ...

BETTINA. <u>Were</u> stupid ... of course ...

JIM. Well, if you were ... oh ... I don't know ... Sometimes I'm not sure whether I'm talking it ... (lowers his voice, whispers, looks around) or it's talking me ...

BETTINA. What time's Jerry coming ...

JIM. Er ... (leans over; looks at his watch lying beside the bed) ... he should be here already ...

BETTINA. Does he know?

JIM. No. (To his foot) Cor, look at that!

BETTINA. You'll have a nice chat, then.

(Silence)

I don't feel like going in today.

JIM.   You don't have to ...

BETTINA.   I don't have to do anything ...

JIM.   Right ...

BETTINA.   I can do exactly as I please ...

JIM.   More or less.

BETTINA.   In that case ...

(Pause. They look at each other)

BETTINA.   In that case ...

JIM.   What ...

BETTINA.   In that case ...

JIM.   Open the bloody thing, for Christ's sake ...

BETTINA.   I think probably ...

(All this time he's been laboriously, delicately, taking off his sock. When he finally gets it off, he examines the foot very minutely. There is nothing to be seen)

JIM.   You think, probably ... ah! ... this little piggy ...

BETTINA.   I think ...

JIM.   I've got that bit ... I could have sworn it was out. It's bloody painful, though, Bettina.

BETTINA.   I think ...

JIM.   Oh, belt up.

43

TINA. I think I'll have it.

(Pause)

I. Oho.

BETTINA. You're not angry?

JIM. Er ... no ... of course not ... why the hell should
I ... you've decided ... okay ...

BETTINA. Yes, I think I have, anyway. Yes. I have. I will
have it. Ha, ha. I feel ...

JIM. Relieved?

BETTINA. I don't know what I feel ... I feel better.

JIM. Morally?

BETTINA. What'll you do?

JIM. Me?

BETTINA. You.

JIM. What'll I do?

BETTINA. Yes.

JIM. Me ... ? Oh ... I don't know ... I was just thinking
something, that's all ...

BETTINA. (affectionately) What were you thinking, o mind!

JIM. I was thinking, Bettina, that you are a stupid, selfish bitch.

BETTINA. Oh ... !

JIM. (stares at her. Says coldly) Oh.

Scene Three

(JIM is sitting on the bed, snoring, staring at JERRY, then at nothing, then at anything. A long silence. JERRY is busy cutting a long, thin strip of paper from a newspaper. He is doing it very neatly. When he's done it he takes the shape and twists it, then joins the ends to form a circle. He holds the ends together. He looks at JIM. Between these two men, beneath the friendship, there is a great deal of latent hostility which, in such a context, easily becomes activated)

JERRY. Have you got any sellotape?

JIM. In the drawer.

(JERRY gets up, goes to a drawer in the sideboard, opens it, looks in it)

JERRY. Where?

JIM. (nodding to a sort of table-desk) That drawer.

(JERRY goes to it, opens the drawer, takes out a sellotape tin. Goes back to his seat. As he does this JIM says)

JIM. How's things?

JERRY. (begins to try to open the tin of sellotape) Okay.

JIM. How's Christine?

JERRY. Who?

JIM. Christine! Your wife!

JERRY. Okay.

JIM. Good ... glad to hear it.

JERRY. (finding the lid difficult, tries his teeth on it.

Mumbles) How are things with you?

Pardon?

RY. Sorry. It's this ... (Tears at it with his nails)

.. That's alright. What are you trying to do?

£RRY. Eh?

JIM. I admire the way you go about things.

JERRY. Uhu ...

JIM. It's very methodical ...

JERRY. Mmmm. Ah. (The tin bursts open)

JIM. Very neat ...

JERRY. It's empty!

JIM. Yes.

JERRY. Well, you haven't got any sellotape, then.

JIM. Yes, it's in the drawer ...

JERRY. Oh ... what's the tin for, then?

JIM. (goes to the drawer) What are you supposed to be doing anyway?

JERRY. I could join it together with glue.

JIM. There's no glue. Here.

(He throws a roll of sellotape to JERRY. Goes back to his bed. Sits on it. JERRY takes a piece of sellotape and bites it off with his teeth. With it he joins the two ends of the strip together. Then puts it down and stares at JIM)

JERRY. Well?

46

JIM. Well what?

JERRY. What are you trying to say?

JIM. Bettina's up the stick.

JERRY. Bettina?

JIM. Christ!

JERRY. Is that the one ... ?

JIM. Push off.

JERRY. So she's up the stick ...

JIM. Yea.

JERRY. Well?

JIM. Need I say more?

JERRY. (takes up the strip and begins to cut around it as if to form two equal strips) Not if you don't want to.

JIM. It's an event of some significance.

JERRY. Possibly.

JIM. To me.

JERRY. Naturally.

JIM. You remember when Christine was up the stick ...

JERRY. Many times ...

JIM. That time, though ...

JERRY. Oh ... yes ... (Puts down the strip)

JIM. That also was an event of some significance.

JERRY. To me.

Naturally.

Y. (takes up the strip) There's a discernable drift to this conversation, if only I could find it ...

You're my friend.

RY. Am I?

M. Yes.

JERRY. (ponders) By all objective tests I suppose I am.

JIM. We've been through a lot together, comrade.

JERRY. Da.

JIM. I was a tower of strength to you, my boy, in your trouble.

JERRY. You got drunk and you were sick all over the carpet.

JIM. I was distressed for you.

JERRY. (puts it down. Meditates) You accused me of being a crypto-fascist and you said the Russians had a rocket aimed straight for my arse.

JIM. That's a grotesque smear on the integrity of the Russian people.

JERRY. When is she primed to go off?

JIM. She says she wants to keep it.

JERRY. They all do ...

JIM. That's what I thought.

JERRY. She's trying it on.

JIM. She's doing that alright ... (Pause) But I'm not having any ...

JERRY. (begins cutting again) No.

JIM. I bloody-well told her. I told her flat.

JERRY. Well done.

JIM. What I said was, if you want it, have it ...

JERRY. That's telling her.

JIM. But you're on your own, I said, all on your own.

JERRY. What did she say?

JIM. Oh, I don't know ... nothing really.

JERRY. Well, what's your problem. To every rational question there is a rational answer.

JIM. I think she'll come round to my way of thinking.

JERRY. Blast.

(He has cut across the strip. He begins, after this, to cut another strip)

JIM. Well, anyway ...

JERRY. (irritably) Blast. Did you give her any of that existentialist guff? Existentialist guff always goes down very well with pregnant women. It's a great comfort to them, that sort of existentialist guff.

JIM. When you and Christine had your first abortion ...

JERRY. (he has cut himself another strip. He gives it a twist. Holds it up) The mysteries of space. Do you know that contrary to an opinion widely held in the West parallel lines do meet ... ?

JIM. Will you listen ... !

JERRY. Alright. (Puts down the strip)

JIM. When you and Christine had the abortion ...

JERRY. I wish you wouldn't keep on saying "you and Christine". Women have abortions. Men do not ...

JIM. Well, what did you do ... ? How did you go about it?

JERRY. Well, first she said she wanted it ...

JIM. Yes ...

JERRY. And I was pleased ...

JIM. You were what?

JERRY. (begins to join up the strip, tearing a piece of sellotape off, etc.) I quite fancied the idea of a little baba ... in a disembodied sort of way ...

JIM. There's nothing disembodied about a little baba, mate ...

JERRY. So I have since found out ...

JIM. It puzzles me how you ever manage to conceive ...

JERRY. The theorem of our desires produces an equation having as its solution a foetus.

JIM. Mathematica Erotica.

JERRY. Yes ... well ... first we thought we'd have it, and then we deduced we wouldn't ... all sorts of reasons, of course, money, family, stupidity, greed, youth ... all that ...

JIM. Yes, so ... get to the practical bit.

JERRY. So I procured for the gentle creature an abortion. The foetus was untimely ripped from her body and slung into a pail.

JIM. Mmm.

JERRY. It occurred to me, brooding on this affair, (he carefully begins to tear the strip to pieces) the thought occurred to me ... this little bloody object which floats all ghastly and dead in the pail ... this ... er ... is all yours ... and ...

JIM. Well, well!

(JERRY is embarrassed by the strength of his feelings, their character, etc. but insists on saying it)

JERRY. It occurred to me that it belonged to me, that I had a sort of umbilical responsibility for this small bit of already decaying matter, that its rudimentary eyes, you follow me, that never saw anything, might, in a metaphysical sort of way, be staring at me and that before all else, as it were, having done nothing particularly good or noble or even just splendid all the days I've been here ... er ..., I might just have ... kept it ... sort of ... how shall I put it ... protected it, from all and sundry, from the bloody medical profession, the doctors ... the knife ... and harm ... the one person who should have been between it and floating in that bucket ... instead of which ...

JIM. Jee ... sus.

JERRY. So these thoughts engendered more thoughts and reinforced a pre-existing disgust I have long held for Western men and all non-Asiatics; me and our lot and all the clever little pale-faced animals in creation, and I thought ... granted the absurdity of the Hindu hypothesis, still, the idea that everything that exists is sacred, does stand between ...

JIM. Holy cow!

JERRY. It being the case, like, Jim, that there's only us and the flies and the world ...

JIM. (offers him some more paper) Have a bit of newspaper.

JERRY. (absent-mindedly takes it. Begins a new strip)
... there's really nothing between us and any sort of
horrible, hideous and hopeless thing you care to
imagine ...

JIM. What I want to know is ...

JERRY. Nothing at all, man, except a feeling ...

JIM. You sentimental mathematical git ...

JERRY. It's a problem to which history provides no solution and Christianity speaks with an ambiguous
voice.

JIM. Bearing all that in mind, et cetera, what I really
want to know is (a) how much is it? (b) where do you
find it? and (c) how long does it take? Facts, that's
what I want. Facts, not ...

JERRY. It'll cost you about a hundred quid.

JIM. As much as that! Er ... I don't suppose ... you ...
I mean, you must have ...

JERRY. (flatly) No.

JIM. Not the whole amount of course. I dare say I could
get something out of the piggy-bank, about 8/4d, and
Bettina could dip her little fingers into her deposit
account ... though I'd rather not ...

JERRY. Does you credit.

JIM. I suppose the N.S.P.C.C. might give us a grant ...
Look, mate ...

JERRY. I can't.

JIM. Well, what do you do with it!

JERRY. I could, but I can't.

JIM. Ah ... scrooples, oh, you got scrooples ...

JERRY. I don't know what I've got but whatever it is, I can't.

JIM. Right. You've said it. Alright ... dee, dee, dee ... I injured myself rather badly today .

JERRY. I can give you an address.

JIM. There's a mate for you ... so far, says Lord Scroople, shall ye go, and not a whit farther. Eh? You were about to speak?

JERRY. Nothing.

JIM. Huh. Well ... The only other outstanding problem is the female thing herself, and ... er ...

JERRY. That's no problem. If you stick to your <u>principles</u> she'll come round to your way of thinking. Women are very malleable.

JIM. I think, Jerry, that you're not responding to the full beauty of my position.

JERRY. I could do with a drink.

(He gets up and looks around)

JIM. I have no intention of <u>forcing</u> Bettina ...

JERRY. Is this gin all there is?

JIM. ... or <u>wheedling</u> Bettina, or doing anything ...

JERRY. Have you got any tonic water?

JIM. ... except make it quite clear to her that in circumstances of this sort ...

JERRY. It's gin and nothing in this establishment ...

JIM. In circumstances of this sort, there are two decisions to make ...

JERRY. Existentialist guff ...

JIM. Two people to decide ...

JERRY. Guff, guff, guff.

JIM. It's better than being a Christian Marxist ...

JERRY. I hope I'm not using your abortion gin?

JIM. For once at least one bloody woman is going to make up her own mind, all on her own ...

JERRY. (takes a drink) This drink is horrible.

JIM. Not, mark you, Jerry, on the assumption that she gets a warm bum to lie down with into the bargain.

JERRY. Some bargain ...

JIM. If she wants it, she can have it ...

JERRY. Are you sure you haven't been pickling things in this?

JIM. That's all she gets. Not me. Just it. I'm here for another purpose.

JERRY. What's that?

JIM. I'm not sure yet.

JERRY. (laughs) Gawd.

JIM. There are, you fool, millions of deaths going on right now ...

JERRY. Deaths do not "go on" ...

JIM. Horrible things are happening this minute ...

JERRY. So?

JIM. So, you're like somebody grieving over the
unbirth of a gnat when there's thousands, getting
burned and blasted and ... all sorts of things are
happening to them ... what about them?

JERRY. It occurs to me, (takes a deep swig of the gin and
begins constructing the new strip)

JIM. Occurs , does it?

JERRY. It occurs to me that people who "grieve" for
what they don't see and don't "grieve" about what's
lying under their noses usually describe those who
do as sentimental gits ... whereas I usually describe
those who reserve their emotions for distant relations
and people beyond the seas as bloody hypocrites or,
putting it another way, as revolting bloody liberals.

(He takes another drink)

JIM. Have a drink.

JERRY. Thank you.

JIM. Anyway, I wasn't talking about feelings. I was talking
about moral issues. What ought to be done.

JERRY. I know what a moral issue is.

JIM. I have a plan.

JERRY. How can you have a plan if you don't know what
it is?

JIM. No, I mean, I have a plan for making it clear to
Bettina that she's on her tod in this ...

JERRY. God is on his tod ... did you know that? Because
he's unique, you see.

JIM. Have you eaten today?

JERRY. If all living objects are sacred, when you decreate
something, you're doing something wrong. That's a
wonderful argument.

JIM. That bloody gin's gone to your head. You're pissed.

JERRY. I'm poisoned ...

JIM. I've got a great plan for isolating Bettina ...

JERRY. Where are those bloody skissors ...

JIM. When I put this plan into operation ... if she still
has it, I'll applaud her integrity whilst regretting her
decision ... from her point of view, of course. As far
as I am concerned the matter is closed.

JERRY. You're not wicked, you're just ignorant. In the
old days you wouldn't have gone to hell. They'd have
had you floating about in the void chatting to the rest
of the don't knows ... You're unreal, man. That's what
ignorance is.

JIM. Pass the gin.

(JERRY passes it)

JERRY. No, now. I know. I know. I know.

JIM. Mmm. I wish we had some tonic.

JERRY. Me, now, I'm damned. At least I would be if there
was any justice in the world.

JIM. Thank God there isn't.

JERRY. Did I put a twist in this strip or not?

JIM. You see, Jerry, what she's got ...

JERRY. Who?

JIM. You drunken bugger ...

JERRY. Oh. (Takes the gin. Drinks)

JIM. (comes close to JERRY. Holds his arm, says quietly) What she's got, man, is hope.

JERRY. (stares at him, incredulous) Hope?

JIM. Yea!

JERRY. Hope!

JIM. Yea!

JERRY. Frying up to me armpits ... (He takes a drink. Rises) Lo ... says the Great Spirit, on his conducted tour of the Shades ...

JIM. She's got this bit of hope tucked away ...

JERRY. ... there, in the coiling pitch, (speaks in a parsonical tone) is one who torments himself ... to whom ...

JIM. At the back of her mind ...

JERRY. To whom, Jim, this boiling pitch is as a balm and a blessing.

(He takes another drink. Throughout JIM's next remark he is taking more gin. Half-way through he stops, puts the bottle down and, looking somewhat surprised, begins to move, very carefully towards the kitchen)

JIM. She's not entirely conversant with the fact but every now and then she gives a sly half glance in its direction ... (glances round at JERRY) there it is, Jerry, a picture.

JERRY. Jim. (Begins to move towards the kitchen)

JIM. ... me and her ... and it, all warm and SNUG and hummy together, daddy and mummy and little cooing and farting Aelfstan ...

JERRY. Jim ...

JIM. It is this social sterotype, Jerry, which governs
      her impulses and her reactions, me and her, she's
      getting a bit fat, you understand?

JERRY. (grimly) Yes ...

JIM. A bit on the plump side but still attractive, mark
      you, the young mother and me ...

JERRY. Jim ...

JIM. Me, Jerry, with me pyjama jacket undone, father
      bear and mother bear and baby bear, the fur
      sprouting from me chest ...

JERRY. I'm sorry, Jim ...

JIM. Yes, good to them both, by God, going to the sea-
      side.

JERRY. Oh ... (looking very ill indeed, has arrive at the
      kitchen sink)

JIM. The British Family Unit, hugger mugger ... (frenzied)
      Christ, I will not be crucified on a kitchen table ...

      (JERRY leans over the sink, groans)

JIM. I will not be hung, drawn and quartered on a pile of
      wet nappies, I will not be somebody who buys absol-
      utely everything at Marks and Spencers.

JERRY. I apologise, Jim.

JIM. What?

      (JERRY vomits into the sink)

JIM. (quietly) Jerry.

JERRY. (groans) What?

JIM. You're a dead loss.

JERRY. What ... (vomits)

JIM. A dead loss.

> (JERRY vomits. JIM stares quietly ahead. Says, as JERRY heaves)

JIM. There's a great deal of pure loveliness in the world if we've only got the eyes and ears to perceive it.

> (JERRY vomits)

JERRY. Damned. That's what I'll be.

> (As JERRY vomits for the last time JIM gets up and begins to tidy the place up. He finds a slip among the rubbish, shakes it out, looks at it. JERRY groans)

JERRY. (pokes his head round the door) Do you have a towel?

JIM. You're not damned, you fool ...

JERRY. A towel?

JIM. Here, wipe your revolting gob on that. (Tosses him the slip) Feeling guilty is a simple evasion of responsibility; it's a low form of cunning. You did the right thing.

JERRY. (wipes his face on the slip) Ta, very much.

JIM. Even if you didn't, one non-baba doesn't constitute an excuse for continuous self-indulgence. Take the stick out of your arse and get going.

JERRY. (shakes out the slip. Broods on it) I think Christine hates me.

JIM. Very reasonable. I hate you as well.

JERRY. It's terrible living with somebody that hates you.

JIM. Everybody hates everybody. It's a terrible world. Only a few of us have the courage to admit it.

JERRY. Terrible, terrible. United in sacred bonds to somebody that loathes the sight of you.

JIM. (gets up, goes to the cupboard, gets out a half-finished bottle of VAT 69 and a couple of glasses, pours out a couple of drinks) Only the very nicest people are capable of admitting how much they hate people. (Takes a swallow) But it's all there, boy, inside every smile, it's twitching about inside every muscle. You can smell it, you can taste it, watch them swallowing it down. Lovely. I think I must be a saint. Here ... (gives him the glass)

JERRY. I thought you said ... (waving the glass)

JIM. I lied....

JERRY. That's alright, then. (Drinks) Ugh. (Meditates) Christine's a hard woman. There's not a soft spot in her.

(JIM picks up a half-completed strip, begins to cut round)

JERRY. She's not like a woman. Her voice isn't gentle, her eyes are not kind. She's not vulnerable ... no ... no ... (Empties the glass, gets up, fills it)

JIM. Hmmm.

(Pause. JIM is concentrating on the strip. JERRY is deducing the following)

JERRY. She's impregnable ... (drinks)

JIM. Hardly that, mate. (Takes a swig of his VAT 69. Pours himself another)

60

JERRY. A fortress, armed to the teeth. At night she goes
out on forays and devastates the countryside. (Drinks.
Pause) That's what she does ... Sometimes I can hear
her laughing when she comes in.

JIM. On her broomstick.

JERRY. Eh?

JIM. You make her sound like a bloody witch.

JERRY. Yes, Jim, she belongs to the Consumers' Assoc-
iation. I'm on her menu. After the soup ... !

JIM. (fiddling with the strip and getting more irritable)
Your mind's diseased. Your brains have gone hay-
wire ...

JERRY. I used to have a lovely brain once ...

JIM. Ugh ... (Still fiddling)

JERRY. Now it's like a broken abacus floating in a bucket of
gin.

JIM. (violently) You've got buckets on the brain.

JERRY. Physical deterioration is bad ... but not as
bad as when you see all the little lights in your brain
going out one by one.

JIM. (lowers the strip. Stares at JERRY) It's selfishness
I dislike most. Somebody, like me for instance, in a
terrible predicament, without a penny piece to his
name, at his wits end, so to speak, and somebody else,
as rich as bloody Croesus, and a putative friend to
boot, sitting there, wiping his rotten face on Bettina's
underwear and continuously intruding his entirely
gratuitous grief on you.

JERRY. (drinks. Waves his glass at JIM) And here's me, a
self-confessed murderer and you coldly compounding
another - something sleeps that will be dead - and I
eat and I'm getting fat, the rats are chewing my hair

61

and I've got no hope.

(From this moment the relationship rapidly deter-
iorates)

JIM. You're only thirty-one, for God's sake ...

JERRY. What's time got to do with it. I'm old enough to
begin to see the holes in the ground.

(JIM takes the strip and makes the final cut, shakes
it out. Instead of falling into two halves as he had
expected it remains one complete shape with a twist
in it. He stares at it. He is immensely irritated and
disappointed)

JIM. And what's this thing supposed to be?

JERRY. (sarcastically, asserting his technical superiority)
It's a topological curiosity, Jim.

JIM. A what?

JERRY. (takes it from JIM. Waves it up and down in
front of him) It's only got one side, you see, Jim.

JIM. No, I don't see.

JERRY. Well, the thing about this strip is it helps you to
understand ...

JIM. Does it? ...

JERRY. Yes, it helps you to grasp how a twisted bastard
like you could, in four dimensions, so to speak ...

JIM. You're trying to tell me something, are you ... ?

JERRY. Put his left hand into his right hand glove ...

JIM. You are trying to tell me, by means of that mathematical montrosity, that you're not exactly one hundred
per cent behind what I'm doing.

JERRY. Far be it from me, mate, to intrude my feelings.

JIM. Your what?

JERRY. Feelings. You know.

JIM. Oh yes. I know all about feelings.

JERRY. Ha!

JIM. I mean feelings are very popular nowadays, everybody's having them, you know, nowadays ...

JERRY. You don't say.

JIM. Yes, I do. They're all having them. They're fash-
ionable things, feelings. Do you know what, o mate ...

JERRY. (puts the strip round JIM's neck) There we are.

JIM. (tears the strip off) I'm absolutely sick to death of
these feelings people are having ...

JERRY. Who's having?

JIM. You ... Bettina. Everybody.

JERRY. I don't think we can help it, Jim. I think it's
something we were born with.

JIM. Even when you don't have them, you scratch away at
yourselves until you do ... It's not YOU that gets
hurt, it's your precious bloody feelings. There you
all are, holding them out, all dripping, for inspection,
all 57 varieties, all held out to dry in the warm sun-
light of public approval.

JERRY. (amused) Perhaps they're worried about Vietnam.

JIM. Who? Who's worried about Vietnam?

JERRY. There's some ghastly things being done out there.

JIM. I know. I know. Everybody's writing about it.

(Declaims)

> What are you doing to me, Vietnam,
> Have you no pity,
> Every day my feelings are lacerated
> By the examination of your artificial sclerosis ...

JERRY. Good. Good.

JIM.

> By your children, lying about in the chicken
> bones,
> Like burnt black plastic ...

(JERRY applauds)

JIM.

> It's a crying shame, Vietnam,
> What you are doing to my feelings.

(JERRY pours himself a drink. Waves it at JIM. JIM holds up his hand for silence)

JIM.

> Vietnam, Vietnam,
> If this goes on
> I shall become so wretched
> My red pen will scorch my finger-tips,
> My feelings will rise up
> To acknowledge the applause.
> Oh Ginsberg! Oh Adrian Mitchell!
> How beautiful, precious and perfect are
> your feelings;
> Pray God, pray Buddha,
> Nothing goes right in Vietnam.

JERRY. Bloody good, Jim. Very moving man. You should publish it in Encounter.

JIM. You bloody hypocrite. You're not worried about Vietnam. Nowadays everybody fancies himself as a sort of Bertrand Schweitzer, concocting world messages from Lambarene or Penryndeudraeth...

JERRY. It's better than Buchenwald or the Berchtesgarten.

JIM. It's just the same - objectively speaking. No doubt
there's much wailing and gnashing of teeth, many
poems get written, many young backsides wear the
print of cold pavements but mark me, Jerry, the
bombs are still falling from Suez to Haiphong and you
are still paying your taxes.

JERRY. You're right, Jim, bloody right.

JIM. You wet-eyed git. You keep on thinking I agree with
you.

JERRY. Oh, I agree with you, Jim. Definitely.

JIM. When I think what I used to think, not so many years
ago ... a society of autonomous legislators in a
kingdom of ends!! And what have we, eh?

(JERRY shrugs)

JIM. I'll tell you, a society dedicated to the proposition
that the lame, the halt and the blind shall inherit
the earth, a society fit for pooves and spastics to live
in.

JERRY. You're trying to annoy me, but I forgive you.

JIM. Ugh ... I've made up me mind. My life henceforth
will be constructed out of a sequence of small,
private acts, breathing, walking, eating and drinking
a bit, getting it when and where I can. I shall learn
the chords and discords of my own character and play
only those tunes which genuinely correspond to some
need in myself. I shall give up slogans, eschew prog-
rammes, I ...

JERRY. You'll die like a rat.

JIM. Possibly ... but maybe that's what I am.

JERRY. No, no, no. You've got a generous nature ...

underneath. Not like some people I could mention ...

JIM. Mmm.

JERRY. You know to whom I refer. You're not like that
woman, Jim. All your badness is the outcome of a
sort of puzzled goodness. (He is very pleased with
this remark) That's the most perceptive thing I've
ever said.

JIM. You're trying to buy my approval ...

JERRY. I didn't know it was for sale.

JIM. You're about as perceptive as a cow staring at a
bottle of milk.

(JERRY gets up. They stare at each other. The
hostility becomes acknowledged. JERRY is upset)

JERRY. Well, what ... what are you then, eh? (He walks
across the room, kicking paper in front of him. Comes
to the bookcase, fingers the cock) What are you ... ?

JIM. What's the matter with you, are you stupid or something
... ?

JERRY. No ... no. (Shakes his head) Not stupid ... not
stupid. (He picks up the cock, shakes it, stares at
it) What's this, then ... ?

JIM. What does it look like?

JERRY. Well ... (stares at it intently, turns it round) ...
a big, glossy, china cock.

JIM. So?

JERRY. That's what it is ... (Grins, waves it about)
Yours?

JIM. Put it down.

JERRY. So that's what you've bought yourself, is it, a

great big, glossy, china cock.

JIM. I've told you.

JERRY. Nice ... really nice ... Jim. A lovely little creature, Jim.

JIM. It's Bettina's.

JERRY. It's what?

JIM. Bettina's ... I bought it for her.

JERRY. Did you ... a sort of ... present ...

JIM. Put it down ...

JERRY. (shrieks suddenly) Cock-a-doodle-doo ... Ain't I Lawrentian ...

JIM. I've told you.

JERRY. So you have, so you have. (Puts it down) There, there ... it's a real beauty ... a real beauty.

JIM. (in concentrated fury) Christine's a wonderful woman ...

JERRY. Yea ... yea. (Blinks)

JIM. Wonderful, wonderful.

JERRY. (defensively) I'll leave you that address. All you do is call round and he'll fix you up ... fix her up ...

JIM. She doesn't give a bugger ...

JERRY. He'll fix you up ...

JIM. You'll not be the last ...

JERRY. He'll have that baba of yours right where you want him ...

JIM. If the present population explosion continues, in ten years we'll be up to our knees in excrement ... wading in our own shit ... Oh God ... !

JERRY. Before he can lisp Jack Wobinson.

JIM. They'll be building cradles out of human excrement, one on top of the other ...

JERRY. Jim ...

JIM. She's shopped around and she won't stop at you ...

JERRY. What are you doing, man?

JIM. She's a tough cookie ... them boots was made for walking ...

JERRY. I have no illusions ...

JIM. God Almighty ... !

JERRY. Not in that direction.

JIM. I've always had a fancy for Christine ... She and me'd suit each other ...

JERRY. She thinks you're something the cat brought in ...

JIM. Those eyes of hers, have you noticed, when there's men around, big, looking ...

JERRY. Stupid, stupid ... (he fumbles for the address)

JIM. What I think I'll do, old mate, is to have Christine round here for a chat ...

JERRY. You're welcome ... you're bloody welcome ...

JIM. We'll be all cosy, me and Christine ... and then Bettina'll come in and that'll be that ...

JERRY. Right ... right ...

JIM. That is the plan.

JERRY. If you and Christine ...

JIM. What?

JERRY. I'll cut her into pieces ...

JIM. Chacun son gout. She is, I suppose, all fixed up?

JERRY. Eh?

JIM. Fixed up ...

JERRY. I have, as a matter of fact, a used condom. Perhaps we could share ...

JIM. How very sophisticated of you.

JERRY. Yes, yes ... I'm going now ... I'm sorry I couldn't manage to spew on your carpet.

JIM. Never mind, you did your best ...

JERRY. Yea ... old mate ... yea ...

JIM. Be seeing you.

JERRY. Yea ... yea ... (He leaves the address and goes)

JIM. Bless you ... Bless you ... (Shouts down the staris) ... and thank you for everything ... for your scrooples ... (Turns, limps back into the room, kicks the paper around, says to himself) ... and your lovely advice and ... everything ... and the meek shall inherit the earth ... they can have it, ouch, my foot.. (Goes to the shaving mirror, bares his teeth in a ferocious grin) Bless you, bless you, my son. You disgust me. You really do. Do I father? That's an improvement, i'n't it, father? We've always approved of ourselves before. Very good.

(He puts the mirror down. Goes to the phone, dials, sings "She was only a bird in a gilded cage")

JIM. Hello ... Christine ... yes ... Jim. Well, thank you, yes, well ... yes ... I've got that old slob of yours here ... yes ... on the carpet ... yes ... would you ... yes ... he's in no fit state ... yes, collect him ... like lazarus, yes ... what ... will you ... what a sweetie you are ... you are ... see you ... yea ... yea ...

ACT TWO

Scene One

(The room is still in a state of confusion although attempts have been made to tidy up the worst of it, the paper, for example, glasses and so on)

CHRISTINE. Where is he ... hiding?

JIM. He's gone.

CHRISTINE. The way you were talking I thought he was lying on the floor in a drunken stupor.

JIM. He was pretty far gone.

CHRISTINE. Hmmm. You're a bad influence on him.

JIM. Serves him right, then.

CHRISTINE. (looking round the room) Men are incompetent.

JIM. Oh?

CHRISTINE. What a wreck this place is.

JIM. I'm not complaining.

CHRISTINE. That's even worse.

JIM. Tidy it up, then.

CHRISTINE. No thank you.

JIM. I'm sorry it's a mess. It's all Jerry's fault really. He seems to spread confusion in a room ... normally it's very tidy indeed.

CHRISTINE. Is It?

JIM. It is. Spic and span.

CHRISTINE. (moves some clothes, sits down) Yes. Of course, some men who live on their own get like that.

JIM. Like what? (CHRISTINE shrugs) Well, that's more or less fixed us, then, hasn't it? If we're not slobs we're pooves and if we're not pooves we're slobs. Poor Jerry.

CHRISTINE. Don't you start feeling sorry for him as well. Everybody feels sorry for Jerry. Jerry is an artist in the art of getting people to feel very sorry for him ... nice, quiet, gentle, intelligent Jerry married to that great, strident, self-assertive virago.

JIM. I like great, strident, self-assertive viragos.

CHRISTINE. I don't and it's not what I am anyway. It's just that if you're married to a minus 10, plus 1 seems a very large number.

JIM. Don't you like being married, then?

CHRISTINE. What sort of question's that?

JIM. I mean, Christine, you've got two really lovely children.

CHRISTINE. Yes. (Grinning at him)

JIM. Don't you like having two really lovely children? I thought it was every woman's ambition to have a nice, steady hubby and two really lovely children.

CHRISTINE. I'm sometimes afraid, Jim, if I lift up my skirt I'll find a little white creature, half blind, called a man, crawling about under it ...

JIM. I see.

CHRISTINE. Were you thinking of getting married, then Jim, old chap. Because chaps of your age who don't get married start to go off, Jim.

JIM. I was seriously thinking of not getting married, old girl.

CHRISTINE. Who's the lucky young creature ... ?

JIM. A tender young bird called Bettina.

CHRISTINE. She must be something for you to think seriously of not marrying her ...

JIM. She's got all the usual features and functions.

CHRISTINE. Have I seen this paragon?

JIM. I think not.

CHRISTINE. You should get married.

JIM. Not bloody likely. Marriage is for women.

CHRISTINE. On the contrary, James, marriage is for men. No sane, intelligent woman should ever contemplate marriage ...

JIM. You think not ...

CHRISTINE. I think not ... any woman that can earn her keep can have the lot, children, a home, undsoweiter, without lumbering herself with some useless, male appendage ... an appendage, moreover, who is convinced it's buying itself martyrdom, a mother, a sister, a mistress, a housekeeper, a life's companion and friend ...

JIM. You're an Amazonian woman, Christine. I can see you Gnadige Frau, striding the camps in your black plastic 'mac and your dugs armoured in steel ...

CHRISTINE. Isn't there anything to drink in this house?
(Takes off her coat. JIM assists. Surprised) Thank
you.

JIM. My pleasure. Shouldn't you be going back to look
after the wife and kids ... ?

CHRISTINE. No.

JIM. Gut. There's a glimmer of gin somewhere, Liebchen,
but I have a notion it's slightly diluted with Jerry's
spit ...

CHRISTINE. Make me some coffee, then.

JIM. To hear is to obey.

(He clicks his heels and goes to the kitchen)

CHRISTINE. You've known Jerry a long time, haven't you?

JIM. Yea. Donkeys years.

CHRISTINE. Was he always a slob, then?

JIM. I beg your pardon. What did you say?

CHRISTINE. I said "was he always a slob"?

JIM. A slob?

CHRISTINE. You heard me.

JIM. Your husband, you mean?

(Silence)

Yes.

CHRISTINE. He must have been a slob when I married
him, then.

JIM. When you married him he was at his highest point of slobdom.

CHRISTINE. I must like slobs, then.

JIM. Actually, at that time, as I remember it, he was concealing his slobdom under a hard shell of wordly cynicism or disgust ... then, in the shelter of your arms, he emerged, with his two horns waving in front of him ...

(CHRISTINE gets up, starts poking around the room, lifting things up, etc. She picks up a tie)

CHRISTINE. Do you actually wear this tie?

JIM. Which tie?

CHRISTINE. This red thing.

JIM. Sometimes. On the Queen's birthday. Why? Do you want to borrow it?

CHRISTINE. This is new, isn't it? (She fingers the china cock)

JIM. What's that?

CHRISTINE. I hardly like to say, darling. Can't you guess?

JIM. Eh ... oh ... the big china cock you mean. Yea.... it's a recent acquisition.

CHRISTINE. Who acquired it?

JIM. Who d'you think?

CHRISTINE. How sweet.

JIM. Actually, I bought it ...

CHRISTINE. Did you?

JIM. (rather irritated) Yes.

CHRISTINE. How sweet.

JIM. (returns with the coffee) Of course, it must be borne in mind, Christine, that big, self-assertive, Amazonian Virago-type girls, adore slobs. Sex-wise. That statement constitutes B. Shaw's sole claim to human insight. Amazing. You've got to admire it.

CHRISTINE. Don't mock Bernard Shaw. He was a great man.

JIM. I love Bernard Shaw. I really do. Good old Bernard Shaw.

CHRISTINE. Are you a slob?

JIM. Nobody that feels like I do about Bernard Shaw ... and H. G. Wells and Aldous Huxley, all those wonderful people ... is a slob.

CHRISTINE. Perhaps I should have married you ...

JIM. It's an ugly but interesting thought.

CHRISTINE. The children adore Jerry.

JIM. Look under that sort of adoration and you'll find something soft, white and horrible ...

CHRISTINE. One teaspoonful.

JIM. Why don't you leave him?

CHRISTINE. He'd disintegrate if I left him.

JIM. Rubbish. The pieces'd just regroup themselves into a rather more doleful pattern. Anyway, who said it was your business to keep him all together?

CHRISTINE. Whose business is it, then?

JIM. His.

CHRISTINE. Anyway, there's the children ...

JIM. That remark is usually the preface to some wildly indecent act ...

CHRISTINE. You'll be lucky ...

JIM. Children, you know, are the new form of quick drying cement. Nowadays wonky marriages are supposed to be stuck together by an application of quick drying children ... Let everything wonk to bits in its own way, that's my motto.

CHRISTINE. Well, you know where you can stick it ... I thought you were his friend ... !

JIM. I was. I am. I'm thinking what's best for him, that's all. And you, lovey. I'm your friend as well.

CHRISTINE. Any friend of Jerry's ...

JIM. No. Really. I think of myself as your friend, Christine.

CHRISTINE. Is that what you think of?

JIM. Darling ...

CHRISTINE. Buzz off.

JIM. Jerry says you think of me as something the cat brought in.

CHRISTINE. Funny boy. He's jealous.

JIM. (holds out his arms) Christine ... I can offer you nothing but blood, toil, tears and wit ...

CHRISTINE. Sorry ...

JIM. I may not be the real thing but at least I'm an absolutely genuine reproduction.

CHRISTINE. I'm very flattered, lovey ...

JIM. Liar ...

CHRISTINE. ... you're not included in my horizon of
    expectations ...

JIM. Ah, well ... tant pis. It's what I anticipated, anyway ...
    you obviously like helpless men. You want to watch
    it, though.

CHRISTINE. Oh?

JIM. Uhu. Helpless men are very dangerous. They're
    woman suckers ...

CHRISTINE. Don't tell me ...

JIM. Women suckers are the most contemporary of men
    ... ! Recognising that we have moved into a new age,
    the Age of the Rampant, Rampaging or Amazonian
    female, each species to be found prowling from Bo'-
    ness to Potter's Bar, from Bonn, Germany, to
    Birmingham, Alabama, your woman sucker also
    recognises that it is the fate of all men, ultimately,
    to be herded into compounds and kept for special
    occasions. To stave off this lugubrious and inevitable
    process they try to draw out, or off, the essence of
    women, suck them into themselves. Their motto is
    "If you can't beat 'em, suck 'em." They're not homo-
    sexual, exactly, or exactly anything; they're more
    like parasites who assume the shape of the hostess
    upon whom they feed.

CHRISTINE. Bravo.

JIM. You're not impressed?

CHRISTINE. I don't think so.

JIM. I like your dress ...

CHRISTINE. Oh come on!

JIM. And I like the way you've done your hair.

CHRISTINE. You're embarrassing me, Jim. What do you
    want?

78

(Pause. They look at each other. CHRISTINE frowns)

CHRISTINE. But I don't know what you want if for. You've never wanted it before.

JIM. How do you know?

CHRISTINE. I know.

JIM. Well, I do now. I feel suddenly that I need to experience you.

CHRISTINE. I don't want to be experienced ...

JIM. Well, aren't you curious about me ... ?

CHRISTINE. I don't know.

JIM. Think about it.

CHRISTINE. I am.

JIM. Well?

CHRISTINE. I don't think I'm very curious about you.

JIM. Well, let's do it coldly, then. Like a couple of sexual experimenters, clinically, diagnostically, observing our own and each other's physical responses.

CHRISTINE. I can't.

JIM. You can. You can, Christine. You can.

CHRISTINE. No ... no.

JIM. Yes.

CHRISTINE. No.

JIM. Why not?

CHRISTINE. I think, probably, because I don't really like you, Jim ... there's something ... not quite right ...

something absent, perhaps ...

JIM. You're quite wrong. Quite, quite wrong.

CHRISTINE. (looks at him) No. There's definitely something ... something I don't really like about you ... Perhaps I ought to experience you ...

JIM. That's what you should do ...

CHRISTINE. Perhaps I ought to do something which I know to be repugnant and outrageous ... perhaps everybody ought to do one really dreadful thing ...

JIM. One really wicked and evil and awful and ghastly thing ... like going to bed with me.

CHRISTINE. Yes, something that so disgusts one, something that's so far at the bottom of the heap that after that anything else one does ...

JIM. My new girl friend's up the stick ...

CHRISTINE. The paragon, you mean! How interesting ... !

JIM. Yes ... she's far gone. My new girl friend has got herself into a predicament.

CHRISTINE. Yes ... I see.

JIM. You don't see anything ...

CHRISTINE. I do ... beneath the noise and the conversation a pattern begins to emerge ... a shape ... a figure ...

JIM. Fat, fish-like and fertile ... I like the way those ear-rings dangle ...

CHRISTINE. Something nasty is crawling about in your mind.

JIM. Will ya, won't ya, will ya, won't ya ...

CHRISTINE. I'm being used for an ulterior purpose ...

JIM. What difference does that make?

CHRISTINE. You're an absolute bloody swine, Jim.

JIM. I'm an absolute bloody swine, Christine.

CHRISTINE. You're totally without scruples.

JIM. I scruple not. Your jawbone is strong but gentle, your eyes fierce but kind.

(He takes her jawbone in his fingers, turns her head and looks into her eyes)

CHRISTINE. I refuse to be used.

JIM. Well, you shouldn't. What's the use of being useless, eh?

CHRISTINE. That's a cheap ... semantic ... trick.

JIM. You're right, of course. (He turns his attention to the zip fastener at the back of her dress) Zip fasteners ... I adore zip fasteners ... I'm a zip fastener fetichist.

CHRISTINE. It's bad. It really is bad ... Geroff...

JIM. Mmmm. When I'm old, when I'm very old, when I'm old, toothless and without sense, I'll lie in a huge, soft bed with a zip fastener ... and I'll zip it up and I'll zip it down ... (does so) and up and down and have pictures of you, Christine, and when I'm very tired I'll close my eyes and mutter your name.

CHRISTINE. You filthy old git ...

JIM. In an old man's high-pitched, senile voice, with me zip fastener dangling from me fingers like a rosary I'll tell the girls I have known and who have known me and that's how I'll go ...

CHRISTINE. And what'll we girls think of, we lucky ones?

JIM. You'll think of me, all the time and you'll be pleased and you'll not know why.

CHRISTINE. You egotistical bastard.

JIM. Me, me, me.

CHRISTINE. Ego-maniac ...

JIM. Virago ...

CHRISTINE. Unromantic, egotistical fornicator ...

JIM. We should, of course, be leaping and running and jumping up and down in the woods ...

CHRISTINE. In slow motion ... !

JIM. Yes, huge, symbolical leaps and bounds and we should fall down ...

CHRISTINE. Look at each other ...

JIM. Laughing and then serious ...

CHRISTINE. With the cameras trained on us ...

JIM. Nothing acts faster than Anadin ...

CHRISTINE. Menthol fresh, my tongue will touch your cheek ...

JIM. We'll have a break, we'll have a Kit-Kat.

CHRISTINE. I like a man

JIM. Who likes it enough

CHRISTINE. (very dramatically) The trees will be above me.

JIM. (in an actor's beautiful, emasculated 1930's voice) Your hair in your eyes, blown across your face ...

82

(As he says this BETTINA comes in. CHRISTINE has her back to her. JIM notices her as he says "Blown across your face.")

CHRISTINE. Your young, brown muscles will bunch against my arm ...

JIM. (looks at BETTINA, says slowly) My girl spreads straight from the fridge ... Hallo ... Did you want something?

CHRISTINE. (turns round ... sees BETTINA, says flatly) Hallo ... (Fastens up her zip)

JIM. Oh, I'm sorry ... Christine this is ...

CHRISTINE. For Christ's sake.

BETTINA. Did you get that address?

JIM. Yes ... er ... he left it on the sideboard ...

BETTINA. Right...thank you.   (Stands there)

JIM. Yes, well ... what about the money?

BETTINA. I don't know ... I don't know ...

JIM. Don't think about it.

BETTINA. I don't know what you're made of ... what sort of thing you are ...

JIM. No ... perhaps not ...

(BETTINA turns and leaves)

CHRISTINE. Well ...

JIM. Well, well ... (sees the address on the sideboard) damn. (Calls down the stairs) Bettina ...

CHRISTINE. Leave her alone.

JIM. Not on your nelly. She's left the address.

(JIM rushes after BETTINA, calling. CHRISTINE, faintly amused, lights a cigarette, reaches for her coat. JIM comes back in, panting)

JIM. I caught her.

CHRISTINE. What did she say?

JIM. Nothing.

(They look at one another)

CHRISTINE. Well, James?

JIM. Well, Christine?

CHRISTINE. That seems to be that.

JIM. You're not going, are you?

CHRISTINE. I think so.

JIM. Stay a bit longer and examine me objets d'art.

CHRISTINE. No.

JIM. Oh, come on. Be pleasant. I've had a hard day.

CHRISTINE. Have you, pet?

JIM. I have, I really have.

CHRISTINE. Aaaah.

(JIM begins to take off his shirt)

CHRISTINE. What are you doing?

JIM. Going to bed.

CHRISTINE. Isn't it a bit early?

JIM. Look, Christine, between you and me and the bedpost, are you or aren't you?

CHRISTINE. I aren't.

JIM. Right then. Good afternoon, madam.

CHRISTINE. Giving up, are you?

JIM. Yes.

CHRISTINE. Well, darling, the trouble is you're such a fertile little creature, I don't think I dare risk it. I mean, what happens if we ... ?

JIM. (begins to unbutton his shirt) Jerry'd look after it.

CHRISTINE. I suppose he would. Isn't that extraordinary.

JIM. Splendid. You're splendid. I admire that.

CHRISTINE. I thought you would.

JIM. Come away with me.

CHRISTINE. Where?

JIM. Anywhere. The Far East. The Himalayas. You on one mountain, me on the other.

CHRISTINE. What'll we do, yodel at each other?

JIM. (begins to take off his trousers) In the night, when the natives are bedded down in their mud huts, we'll creep down into the valley and practise co-habitation.

CHRISTINE. Won't you catch cold?

(He removes his trousers. Stands before her)

You think you're beautiful, do you?

JIM. You're beautiful, Christine.

(Moves to beside her. Begins to unzip her dress)

CHRISTINE. Do you think so?

JIM. Very, very, very beautiful. And cruel, and cold, and horrible, and splendid.

CHRISTINE. What about Jerry?

JIM. Never heard of him. This zip fastener could do with oiling.

CHRISTINE. (puts out her cigarette. Looks at JIM) Greater love hath no man ...

JIM. Than to lay down his wife for his friend.

(CHRISTINE gets up. JIM hops onto the bed and wriggles himself down into it)

CHRISTINE. Ah, well ...

JIM. (maliciously, now that he is successful) Jerry says he wanted his baba and you wanted to do it in.

CHRISTINE. Jerry's a liar.

JIM. Ah! You wanted it then.

CHRISTINE. No.

JIM. Mmmmm.

CHRISTINE. Jerry wanted it when he didn't have it and when he didn't have it he was glad. Poor Jerry ...

JIM. Switch the light off.

CHRISTINE. (sits on the edge of the bed. Stares at JIM) I don't like you, Jim.

JIM. No?

CHRISTINE. I think you're rather dreadful.

JIM. I don't care.

CHRISTINE. Neither do I.

JIM. Switch the light off then.

CHRISTINE. Why, does it embarrass you?

JIM. I can't lie here with a hundred watt bulb glaring into me eyeballs.

CHRISTINE. Shut them, then.

JIM. No. You shut yours.

CHRISTINE. No, thank you. I want to see what I'm doing.

Scene Two

(The same. With JIM and JERRY. The room now being prepared for some sort of party, a celebration perhaps. JERRY is squatting on the bed, doing nothing at all, following JIM's actions at most with his eyes. JIM is very busy, preparing the table, going out getting crisps, bowls, glasses, etc. He glances at JERRY occasionally)

JIM. Are you comfortable?

JERRY. Alright.

JIM. You don't look very comfortable.

JERRY. Well, I am. I'm ruminating.

JIM. May one enquire the theme of these ruminations?

JERRY. No.

JIM. Okay. (Gets on with the preparations) We need some more booze ...

JERRY. It was raining when I came in.

JIM. Three more bottles should do it.

JERRY. Cats and dogs ...

JIM. What do _you_ think ... ?

JERRY. Mmmm?

JIM. Do you think I should get three bottles or four bottles?

JERRY. I don't know.

JIM. Three should be enough. (Looks at the table) Not bad, eh?

JERRY. Very nice.

(Pause)

JIM. (looks at JERRY) You're huffed, aren't you?

JERRY. I'm not in the least huffed.

JIM. What are you sitting like that for then?

JERRY. This is known as the seventh position ...

JIM. I thought I knew all the positions. I don't know whether to feed you or open you. (Stares at him, touches him) What's this bit, a leg?

JERRY. If you're going for that booze ...

JIM. (returns to the table, opens a bottle of whisky, VAT 69) Do Gurus drink? (No answer) Ah well. Here's to oriental inscrutability. Here, Mahatma, have a bowl of rice crispies.

JERRY. Thank you.

JIM. (irritated) Thank you. I'm going to get absolutely slewed tonight. Did you say it was raining?

JERRY. Cats and dogs.

JIM. (reaches for his raincoat) Right.

JERRY. Human beings do stupid things.

JIM. True.

JERRY. I was just thinking ...

JIM. Yes ... ?

JERRY. The rain reminded me ...

JIM. (sits down, pours himself another glass) Yes ... ?

JERRY. I was looking out of the window today ...

JIM. Interesting ... ?

JERRY. There was nothing to see, just the other side
of the street and a few cars ...

JIM. Keep them in, rain ...

JERRY. Who?

JIM. I don't know ... Birds. They don't like getting their
feathers all soggy. Stops them flying.

JERRY. Nonsense.

JIM. That's what I heard anyway.

JERRY. The kids were playing in the back room ...

JIM. Noisy things, kids.

JERRY. No, they weren't bad.

JIM. Well trained. Disciplined. Christine ... (Stops)

JERRY. They were making a bit of a racket ...

JIM. Jerry ...

JERRY. Anyway, I was staring out of the window ...

JIM. Okay. (Makes to get up)

JERRY. It just looked like hundreds of little colourless
tadpoles ...

JIM. What did?

JERRY. Running down the window ...

JIM. Tadpoles, eh.

JERRY. It reminded me ...

JIM. When you and me was a couple of little colourless
tadpoles. A lot of rain's run down the window since
that time, mate.

JERRY. When I was miserable I used to sit looking out of
the window and it was always raining ...

JIM. Buckets and buckets of it.

JERRY. I used to think if only I could think what they looked
like ...

JIM. The tadpoles?

JERRY. Yes. If I could do that, it'd be interesting and
then I wouldn't be so miserable ...

JIM. Jerry.

JERRY. Yea.

JIM. Give it up, mate.

JERRY. Give what up?

JIM. It's just bloody rain.

JERRY. Yea, that's what it is.

JIM. It's just bloody rain, so don't go making little tadpoles out of it.

JERRY. What're you going to do now ... ?

JIM. Don't know ... get out of it, I suppose ... I've
had this place anyway ... (Makes a gesture) I have
exhausted its possibilities ...

JERRY. Is that what you've done ... ?

JIM. Yes, Jim's about to emerge, come forth ...

JERRY. Perhaps you should get yourself a little card and
go round offering yourself to the housewives of
Britain ...

JIM. I might, I might; sexual services incorporated ...

JERRY. Jim ...

JIM. Yea?

JERRY. I think you'll only need three bottles ...

JIM. Oh ... yea ... right ... I'll be off then ...

(Grabs his raincoat)

JERRY. (gets up, goes over, pours himself a drink) Cheers.

JIM. Cheers, mate. (Goes)

(JERRY sits on the table, drinks, gets up, restless,
helps himself to a crisp, goes over to the china cock,
lifts it up, examines it, puts it down, sits down,
munches a crisp. BETTINA comes in. JERRY gets
up, holding his bag of crisps)

BETTINA. Where's King Tut off to, then?

JERRY. He's gone out to get some more booze.

91

(Pause)

Have a crisp.

BETTINA. (shakes her head) And what's all this then?

JERRY. I dunno ... he spoke of a party.

BETTINA. I think he must be mad.

JERRY. Is it ... er ... your ... er ...

BETTINA. Yes.

JERRY. I'm sorry.

BETTINA. Oh, I don't know ...

JERRY. I was sorry about ... what happened ... Christine
and ... nothing happened, you know ... not really
... nothing of any importance, that is ... she ... er
... assured me of that.

BETTINA. Oh, good. It's quite a spread, isn't it?

JERRY. Yes. Otherwise ...

BETTINA . Yes.

JERRY. Anyway ... there's the children, you see ... you
have to believe the best ...

BETTINA. Jerry?

JERRY. (scared) What?

BETTINA. Why do you bother with him?

JERRY. I dunno ... he's honest, I suppose ...

BETTINA. Yes.

JERRY. Anyway ... I like him.

(Pause)

BETTINA. How did you and Christine meet?

JERRY. (relaxes) Oh ... I can't remember ... I think it
was at a party ... yea ... there was this great big
stunning blonde ... I was a virgin before I met
Christine.

BETTINA. (amused) Were you really?

JERRY. Yea ...

(They look at each other. He laughs)

Yea, I was the most unpromising virgin of my year. In
fact I was voted the virgin least likely to succeed ...

BETTINA. Fancy!

JERRY. Anyway, at this party, this great, big stunning
blonde comes at me, as it were, and before I could
square the hypotenuse, I was projected onto an inclined
plane and done.

BETTINA. Poor Jerry.

JERRY. No, I enjoyed it. Anyway, so after that she had
to marry me ... at least after the ...

(Pause)

BETTINA. How long do you think he'll be?

JERRY. Well, he's just gone round the corner.

BETTINA. What was Christine like ... ?

JERRY. When? ... Oh ... he told you, did he? He
would, of course. I asked him not to. Yes. Oh,
well, she was a bit distressed ... we both were ...

BETTINA. Is he distressed?

JERRY. I shouldn't bank on it.

BETTINA. He's a lunatic ...

JERRY. Yea ... are you ... ?

BETTINA. (goes over to the bookcase. Picks up the china cock) I just came back for this.

JERRY. Oh, yes, the ... I noticed it ... it's very fine ...

BETTINA. Yes. He's nice.

JERRY. Yes, he is.

BETTINA. Perhaps I ought to leave it, though ...

JERRY. Oh ...

BETTINA. I don't suppose he'll come to any harm ...

JERRY. No ... well ... listen ... if you're alright ... if you don't mind ... I'll be getting along ... I'll be seeing you later at the ... (nods at the table) ... tell Jim ... no ... (Goes up to her, pecks her cheek) Listen, if you want anything, you know ... you can always ring Christine ... or me, even ... the number's in the book ...

BETTINA. Thank you.

JERRY. Right, well, be seeing you.

BETTINA. Yes.

JERRY. Look after yourself.

BETTINA. Yes, yes.

JERRY. Bye.

BETTINA. Bye.

(He goes. She moves round the room. Looks rather

as if she is going to weep)

JERRY. (reappears) Listen ... he's a bastard ... but he's not a _bad_ bastard.

BETTINA. Goodbye.

JERRY. I thought I'd say that. Goodbye.

(He makes to go. He is prevented by the arrival of JIM, who is somewhat drunk)

JIM. Got you. Skulking away, were you ... ?

JERRY. I have to get back, Jim.

JIM. No, you don't. You'll stay with me and Bettina ... won't he, Bettina ... ?

BETTINA. If he wants to go ...

JERRY. I think I ought to ...

JIM. No, you oughtn't. You ought to stay, oughtn't he, Christine ... ?

BETTINA. (quietly) I don't know.

JERRY. That's Bettina.

JIM. Christ; of course it's Bettina. You don't think I'd mistake my little bride of Christ for Horst Wessel's sister, do you ... ? Look what I've got ... (Shows champagne bottles)

JERRY. Yea ...

JIM. Is that all you can say? It's the best ... It's the best that money can buy. Nothing's too good for my baby ... my living doll ... eh?

JERRY. You're pissed!

JIM. I'm what?

BETTINA. You're drunk.

JIM. So what.

BETTINA. It's unpleasant ...

JIM. Offensive, is it?

BETTINA. Yes.

JIM. You don't like me when I'm drunk.

JERRY. Well, I'll just get along.

JIM. The "ought" people don't like me when I'm drunk.
Well, that's very sad. That's the saddest thing today.
The "ought" people hate drunks and layabouts and
no-gooders and all that ... and yet ... don't sneak
off, Jerry, my old friend, my good friend ... and
you don't go either, Bettina ... because what you
both don't realise is that I'm not a cruel man ... I'm
a good man ... a lovable man.

JERRY. Perhaps ...

JIM. Shush ... I'm talking ... I'm saying things ... It's
rude to talk when people are talking ... don't you
know that ... ?

BETTINA. You're being stupid.

JIM. Ah, do you think so?

BETTINA. Yes.

JIM. That's just one person's opinion ... What I'm trying
to tell you and he'll confirm it ... won't you, boy,
you'll confirm it, right up to the hilt ...

JERRY. What?

JIM. You'll confirm to this gallant little woman that above
all else her cavalier and true knight is an honest
man, a true man ... isn't that right ... eh ... eh?

(BETTINA and JERRY stand, looking miserable)

JIM. Sit down now, sit down ...

JERRY. Well ...

BETTINA. Alright.

(They sit)

JIM. You see, people, nobody understands me ...

BETTINA. Oh, my God ...

JIM. (to JERRY, as to an audience) There, there, what did I say, I'm NOT UNDERSTOOD ... Sir, I am not understood ... The first apostle and martyr of freedom and honesty, the first saint of unbelief, the first ... yes ... you may shake your heads; you'll weep before morning, the first solitary man martyred on the sentiments of others. Pray for me, pray for me, St. Sartre, (He looks at JERRY) St. Simone, (Looks at BETTINA) pray for me, all who went before and prepared my way ... Kierkegaard; I believe in me because I am impossible ... the chairs are ludicrous, do you understand me now, the champagne is preposterous ... ah, but ... my love, we'll live a holy life, you and me ... (He kneels to BETTINA)

BETTINA. Your breath smells ...

JIM. (crawls over to JERRY) My true, honest and fearful one ... Now you've been through the fire, (Crawls back to BETTINA) you, I mean, now you've been through the purgatory of being human ... (He twists at a champagne cork) take this booze - (The cork comes out. He gets up) which is my fizzing blood ... (He fills two glasses which he hands to JERRY and BETTINA) ... and this toast and caviare - (He gives them a piece of toast and caviare) which is my crawling body ... together we will roll down the alimentary canal of life and out of the anus of history ... (He takes a drink himself - sprinkles BETTINA and JERRY and the room with drops of champagne) I anoint thy breasts, thy armpits, thy thyroids, with holy oil ... and this ark of the covenant, I anoint it with holy oil ...

BETTINA. For God's sake ...

JIM. (he sits down, drinks, says in an American accent) I hold these truths to be self-evident, that the faith and works of Trumbull Stickney, Ralph Waldo Emerson Louella Parsons, J. Edgar Hoover and (He becomes very solemn, hushes his voice) John F. Kennedy ... shall not pass from the face of the earth.

JERRY. Jim ...

JIM. (jumps up. Waves his arms) All together ... Irish nuns and lean and tasty, Irish nuns are lean and tasty ...

JERRY. Jim ...

JIM. What sayest thou, oh, Christy Marxist man?

JERRY. I'm going. (He goes out)

JIM. Then, begone and may the blessing of God Almighty go with thee ... (Shouts) and yours ...

(JIM comes back into the room. Sits down. Looks at BETTINA)

JIM. (quite seriously) How are you?

BETTINA. What do you think?

JIM. You feel awful.

BETTINA. No, no, I don't. It's nice of you to think so, though ...

JIM. I'm a sentimentalist at heart. From arsehole to breakfast time, my heart bleeds for thee. Drink ...

BETTINA. Caviare as well. It's incredible! (She begins to

98

take off her coat) Help me off with my coat.

JIM. What?

BETTINA. My coat.

JIM. Sorry ... it cost me a fortune.

BETTINA. It's a wonderful gesture.

JIM. I'm glad you see it like that.

BETTINA. I feel like ...

JIM. Don't tell me. You'll only make me feel embarrassed.

BETTINA. I feel like making a wonderful gesture back ...

JIM. (goes towards her) It's nice to see you again, though.

BETTINA. Two days is a long time. Let's drink to something.

JIM. What'll we drink to?

BETTINA. I don't know. It was your idea to have a party ...

JIM. Right ... er ...

BETTINA. What's the matter?

JIM. I don't know. I just can't find the right sort of words to fit the sort of occasion we're supposed to be celebrating ...

BETTINA. I've never known you to be stuck for words before, Jim.

JIM. Give me a chance. I've had half a bottle of whisky already ... near enough ... it's all roaring in my head ...

BETTINA. Perhaps there aren't any words for the sort of

occasion we're supposed to be celebrating...

JIM. If I sit quiet a minute, they'll come ...

BETTINA. Perhaps it's because you're feeling ashamed or
something.

JIM. What was that word?

BETTINA. Ashamed ...

JIM. Oh, yes, ashamed ... possibly ... perhaps ... yes
... it's just as if somebody was pouring the Atlantic
ocean in one ear and it was gushing out of the other ...

BETTINA. Or sorry for something ...

JIM. What, for instance?

BETTINA. I don't know ... perhaps you trod on something
... perhaps your id is a Hindu or something...

JIM. (in Peter Sellars' Indian) Don't talk to me about
Hindus ... don't do it ... Hindus ... it's a way of
life I can't abide ... okay ...

BETTINA. I don't know what it is, then.

JIM. (indignantly) Neither do I ... perhaps, swishing in
drink as I am, ill and likely to vomit at any second,
perhaps it is that in such a moment the normal proc-
esses of social indoctrination, to which I was submitted
in my early years, have, once more, for the moment,
taken hold of me. I have a feeling for you. Did you
not know? So when I saw you standing there ...

BETTINA. Standing?

JIM. Sitting then, what does the posture matter - anyway,
standing, sitting, all defoetalised, looking all white
and shattered, I felt, for the moment, a slight moral
dizziness ...

BETTINA. Poor James ...

JIM. I doubted, for a second, the absolute recititude of my position, I felt a slight twinge of remorse, as function, no doubt, of my social training and my intrinsically generous nature. The contrast between your woebegone face, staring at me like an accuser ...

BETTINA. Is that how it looks?

JIM. ... and me, standing here, with a bottle in me hand ... for the moment ... my sang-froid ... did a sickening lurch ... for the moment I regretted .. things ...

BETTINA. Oh, I shouldn't do that, lovey ...

JIM. You're hard, Bettina.

BETTINA. What?

JIM. Hard ...

BETTINA. God Almighty!

JIM. Anyway, we'll drink this bottle ... eh ... the two of us ... before the others come ...

BETTINA. What others ... ?

JIM. Oh ... I don't know ... Jerry, of course, and his jack-booted wife.

BETTINA. Oh yes ...

JIM. Yes, yes ... and a few other well-wishers ...

BETTINA. Ugh ... !

JIM. I'm glad you're back.

BETTINA. Good.

JIM. I mean it. I'm pleased to see you.

BETTINA. A toast, then ...

101

JIM. Okay ...

BETTINA. To us ...

JIM. Marvellous ... the very cliche.

(They drink)

BETTINA. I've bought you a present.

JIM. Thank you, dearie.

BETTINA. I thought to myself ...

(She pours herself a drink)

... cheers ...

JIM. Cheers ...

(He goes to the table and gets himself a piece of something)

BETTINA. I thought to myself ... "I'll buy old darling Jimmy a present" ... so I did.

JIM. Good for you, pet.

BETTINA. I went right in and I bought you a present.

JIM. You shouldn't have.

BETTINA. Why not?

JIM. Cheers.

BETTINA. Don't you think I ought to have bought you a present ... I mean ... all this ... this wonderful ... gesture ... this ...

JIM. (angrily) If you've come back ...

BETTINA. It's in my bag.

JIM. I was pleased to see you.

BETTINA. Yes? It's a very nice present.

JIM. You're behaving abominably.

BETTINA. Very, very nice. Cheers.

JIM. I said I was pleased to see you.

BETTINA. Why?

JIM. I don't know "why". I just was. I was looking forward
to your coming back.

BETTINA. Ah ...

JIM. Well, I was. I bloody was. Now I begin to perceive.
...

BETTINA. The present I bought you's in my bag ...

JIM. I begin to detect an underground hostility all ready
to come up and join the regular troops ...

BETTINA. This gesture of yours ...

JIM. Bang, bang.

BETTINA. It was an ugly gesture ...

JIM. Bang.

BETTINA. Why did you, then?

JIM. Cheers ... I was pleased to see you ...

BETTINA. It's a sort of wake ... that's what it is.

JIM. Well, you, at least, seem to be in mourning ...

BETTINA. Where's your black arm-band, then?

JIM. I'm not in mourning. Nobody's died ... nobody of

mine. And it was your bloody legs, let me remind you, your lovely limbs, lovey, that walked you ...

BETTINA. Cheers, then ... lovey ...

JIM. Walked you, trot, trot, from here to there. Don't look at me in that accusing tone of voice ...

BETTINA. You manoeuvred me, Jimmy.

JIM. I did what ... ?

BETTINA. You manoeuvred me ...

JIM. I didn't ... you fool ... you fool ...

BETTINA. It doesn't matter ... it's all down the drain ... whatever he, she or it was ... it's all done and finished and over ...

JIM. Cheers, then ...

BETTINA. Cheers ...

JIM. Where did you say that present was?

BETTINA. In my bag.

JIM. Right.

BETTINA. It's hard to live with anybody as remorseless as you ...

JIM. No, it's not. It's easy. You just do what you like and I do what I like and when we coincide it's known as happiness, felicity, or bliss ... ! (He is rummaging in the depths of the bag ... concentrating on that, rather than on what he's saying) Where in your bag?

BETTINA. Right at the bottom ...

JIM. I'm a bit at a loss ... (He feels something) I can't quite understand ... (His expression changes) why ... on what impulse ... (He begins to withdraw his hand

... he looks slightly sick, almost apprehensive) ... what made you ... (He brings out his hand a red colour) ... buy me a present.

(They look at each other)

Because normally, girls ... don't buy chaps ... presents ... Bettina ... my pet ... (He puts his hand on her shoulder)

(She shudders)

What a lovely thing ... (He kisses her) You abominable woman.

BETTINA. You beastly man.

(He releases her. She sits down. He goes to the kitchen, begins to wash his hands)

JIM. Is it, my love, a rabbit or a hare?

BETTINA. (flatly) Rabbit.

JIM. (comes in, drying his hands) Good. I prefer rabbit.

BETTINA. Yes. I remembered.

JIM. I find the taste and smell of hare slightly too... how shall I say ... self-assertive, too aggressive, perhaps ...

BETTINA. I know just what you mean.

JIM. There's blood on your dress.

BETTINA. Is there?

JIM. On your shoulder. (He goes up to her) People you hate ... (He fingers the fabric on her shoulder) because of yourself, you should keep away from ... you'll find them ...

BETTINA. Too self-assertive ...

JIM. Too aggressive, perhaps.

BETTINA. Aren't you sorry about anything ... not one, small, slight, tiny, little thing ... not ...

JIM. No ... no ... I don't think so. Sad, a bit, as always. No. (Thinks) A bit, maybe, about Christine ...

BETTINA. (sarcastically) Yes, that wasn't very nice ...

JIM. I'm not sure why ... It's hard work being a hero.

BETTINA. Is that what you are?

JIM. I hope so.

BETTINA. So do I ... (She goes over to her bag)

JIM. What're you doing?

BETTINA. (she begins to take things out) That damned rabbit ...

JIM. You can unpack later.

BETTINA. Yes. (Takes out the rabbit. It is wrapped in a piece of paper; it is not skinned yet) One defunct bunny. From me to you.

JIM. Ta.

(He doesn't take it. She lays it down)

BETTINA. I should cook it pretty soon. (She begins to put her stuff back in the bag. Puts on her coat) Otherwise the place is going to get pretty high!

JIM. What are you doing?

BETTINA. Pretty stinky poo!

JIM. I'm not really offended ...

BETTINA. The pong can get real bad ...

106

JIM. I'd like you to stay.

BETTINA. Pretty bloody high!

JIM. It's lonely sitting here with the bottles on the table and bits of toast ...

(She buttons up her coat)

and fish eggs ... eh ... Bettina?

BETTINA. No, thank you.

JIM. No?

BETTINA. No.

JIM. Right.

BETTINA. I'll leave you this ... (The rabbit) as a souvenir.

JIM. You can stuff it, as far as I'm concerned.

BETTINA. Too big.

JIM. Oh, I don't know.

BETTINA. Ours was ...

JIM. (defiantly) What?

BETTINA. (shouts) Smaller ...

JIM. (very upset, disconcerted, frightened, angry) Smaller? Smaller? You're crazy. You're insane.

BETTINA. (picks up the rabbit) Here ... (tries to give it to him. He backs away) here, take it.

JIM. I don't want it. What's the matter with you?

BETTINA. (in tears) Take it, I say ... it's yours ...

JIM. I don't want it. Bettina ...

BETTINA. Alright ... alright (Throws it on the floor) alright. (She rushes out)

JIM. Bettina. That was bloody callous. (Kneels down, examines the rabbit. straightens out its legs, etc) ... poor bloody thing. Smaller? Bloody, bloody, bloody insane ... bloody callous. (Gets up with the rabbit) Damn and blast you, Bettina. Damn and blast you and your rotten, stinking ... (Stands, silent, holding the rabbit. Looks around. Breathes in. Recovers himself)

Well ... well ... well ... oho ... little Jim pours e'self, salutes e'self, declares before nobody that he never did nothing, stands accused but won't plead guilty, declares the judges to be of unsound mind, the jury to be confirmed nitwits.

(Looks in the direction of the cock, sighs, goes over to it)

We've got a proper bloody menagerie here.

(Brings the cock to see the rabbit)

Do you know what this is? It's a rabbit. It's a lepus cuniculus, or common burrowing rodent of the hare family. Yes. That's what it is.

(Looks at the rabbit, measures it, opens his eyes wide)

What's size got to do with it? How big? That big? Eh? Ah, well. And what about you, bunny. Nobody asked your permission, did they, cropping away at your greens. They're all for that, aren't they ... bang, bang, bang. Stuff 'em all, say we, eh bunny, women, farmers, the lot. All the lot of them.

(He moves to the tape-recorded, switches it on, climbs on to the bed, lays the rabbit down gently beside him, scratches its ears. Stares ahead, as the music begins quietly)

Ephemoptera! May flies to you, bunny. You must have
seen them. They rise up, in pyramids, on warm
summer nights, propagate, and then die. Huh. Ephemoptera! From the latin; meaning ephemeral; short-
lived. That is the sum total of human wisdom, eh,
big ears. Sad, me furry old mate, but true.

(He settles down, eyes open. The music roars out the
exultant last bars of the 9th Symphony, the choir
shouting "Freude". He stretches, leans carefully over
the rabbit, switches off the light. The music plays, he
begins to snore)

THE END

DEAR JANET ROSENBERG, DEAR MR. KOONING

DEAR JANET ROSENBERG, DEAR MR. KOONING was first performed at the Traverse Theatre Club, Edinburgh, on 1st July, 1969 with the following cast:

ALEC KOONING   Anthony Haygarth

JANET ROSENBERG   Sue Carpenter

The play was directed by Max Stafford-Clark.

ACT ONE

Scene One

(ALEC KOONING and JANET ROSENBERG sit back
to back, each at a desk. It is here they write their
letters to each other. They each have a table-lamp
which, when switched off, plunges their side of the
stage into darkness. JANET's part of the stage is
appropriate to the study-bedroom of a young girl;
ALEC's to a man of his years and degree of supposed
success. They sit in swivel chairs, so that when they
spin round they face each other. It is left to the
director and the free play of ingenuity of the two
actors what they do while the other is reading out a
letter - perhaps action as a counter-point to the state -
ment of the letter or something appropriate to it.
Certainly the author gives little indication of what is
required, no doubt influenced, somewhat belatedly, by
recent trends in the theatre) *As if reading it thro'*

JANET. April 4th. Dear Mr. Kooning. I've just finished
reading your latest book and I feel I have to write to
you to say how very much I enjoyed reading it. I am
nineteen myself and I think it is marvellous the way
in which you seem to get into the mind of somebody
my age. That is what we are like and it is marvellous
to feel for once, that somebody understands us. Of
course I know you must get hundreds of letters like
this but it doesn't matter I just have to write to say
"thank-you" and to say how much I admire what you
have written. Yours sincerely, Janet Rosenberg.

(ALEC KOONING picks up his pen, delighted to
receive this missive and begins to write. As he
writes he speaks the letter)

ALEC. May 9th. Dear Miss Rosenberg, Thank-you for
your kind letter. I'm so glad you liked my latest book,
and particularly delighted that my young readers feel
I have not done them an injustice. I do get many letters,
yes, but I am always delighted when one of the generation of new readers - I suppose I can say you are
that - finds something worthwhile in what I write.
It makes one feel one is in touch with the future.
Best wishes, A. Kooning.

JANET. Nov. 11th. Dear Mr. Kooning, I hope you will
forgive me for writing to you again. After I got your
letter I went straight out and got all your books from
the library and started to read them from end to end.
After I'd read them all, starting with "Blighted
Summer" and going on to "A Savage Hour", "The
Hope of Our Time" and "A New Defeat", I finished
with your last book but one "Against the War" and
then I understood, suddenly, what you were getting at
in "The Hope of Youth" in a much deeper way than
I had before. Today is the 11th of November, Armistice
Day. I had two minutes of silence in my room, the
clocks stopped ticking and even the birds outside my
window stood stock-still to attention in the trees and
didn't whistle. No. I exaggerate. But I felt that's
how it should be. Oddly enough, it's my birthday too
and suddenly this conjunction made me feel I had
to write to you again. Today I am twenty and it seems
to me an awfully significant age to be. Some girls are
all bunged up with babies by now, poor things, and
are indistinguishable from real adults. Well, up to
now I've managed to escape the hazards of conception
so far, Mr. Kooning, being a writer you will know
what I mean, but today I too feel indistinguishable
from a real adult, quite mature in fact, and quite up
to writing to a distinguished man of letters and wasting
his time with idle chatter. But something in what I
want to say to you, Mr. Kooning, is not idle but I
can't say what it is. Something like, I do feel adult
today and that I start my twentieth year full of your

As if doing something else

thoughts. I understand so much now of the sadness of
what is always lost, the people who have died, the
people who should have lived longer, as I hope to do,
and there they all are, stretched out under hundreds
and hundreds of little white crosses, for ever and ever,
amen. I'm not religious, by the way. I don't know
really what I want to say to you, Mr. Kooning, I
only know that I feel that what you have written is
very important to me. Thank-you. Yours gratefully,
Janet Rosenberg.

(A suggestion. There is no reason why JANET should
not be doing something entirely at odds with what she
is saying, or doing something entirely unconnected
with her speaking the letter. She can read a book,
go to bed, brush her hair, dust, arrange her wardrobe ... oddity must be the keynote, incongruity)

warm, with humour

ALEC. 13th November. Dear Miss Rosenberg, Such dark
thoughts for such a young girl. I don't know that in-
sinuating my middle-aged, sephulchral, crepuscular
imagery into the mind of such a young, female person
is a good idea. Such dark thoughts, Miss Rosenberg,
and on your birthday too! My good wishes for that,
by the bye. I've been twenty plus such a long time now,
I've almost, though not quite, lost the feeling of WHAT
A RESPONSIBILITY it all is. Crikey, when you have
had the temerity and pluck, he said, with a gay laugh
and twinkle in his eye, to get through to where I am
now, it's all rather like trying to run backwards. Instead
of getting more serene, more serious, I find myself,
alas, getting more frivolous and flippant every day.
Leaning over a dark precipice in the middle of the
night, seeing, so far below, the white, glinting
bones of preceding travellers - there's a moon, you
understand - all you want to do is to turn tail and run
like anything back to where all the high jinks are
happening. No, I'm only joking, really. It's just that
I'm not at all sure I relish the feeling of responsibility
your letter gives me. Every now and then, being a
writer becomes an awful, pendulous burden, sending
one's thoughts into the world like dry seeds on the
wind, as it were, to fall, one knows not whither. Your
youth, your young vigour, your incipient hopefulness,
your ...

115

As if he were reflecting after the letter –
more personal + passionate.

(He drops his pen, or whatever, turns to JANET,
addresses her back passionately)

Oh, Miss Rosenberg, Janet, twenty, you say ... oh,
my God, and reading my books all tucked up in your
little warm bed! ... Janet, Janet ... what a lovely
cool and plangent sound that is, I'm filled to the tops
of my ears with lust and longing. Twenty, you say, and
all tucked up in bed, with two pillows behind your
head, and your long, golden hair, all drenched down
those pillows and your feet resting like two snoozing
doves on your furry, yellow, hot-water bottle, and
the tips of your fingers caressing ... oh, Janet,
Janet, you don't know what it is like, being fifty,
still full of it, marooned in a cold life, and your
warm little letters dropping like sweet smelling
petals on my carpet ...

(He swivels back to his desk, takes up his pen, or
what-have-you, reads back a few words in his passionately discontinued letter and goes on)

your ... er ... your moment of infinite possibility
how it strikes and wounds, yes, I suppose it does,
someone at the dark, lantern end of life. What a
feeble light to cast in your way. The war I was in, yes,
it was terrible, but, you know, I remember it with a
sort of longing, all one's friends, all that affection
and pain, all gone, all finished now, and now only the
words remain ... words, words, words ... yes,
silence ... two minutes silence ... silence for the
dumb craters ... But yes, be hopeful on your 20th
birthday. It is the time for that. Best wishes, Alec
Kooning.

(He sits there, then crumples the letter up in his
hand, casts it down on the floor under the desk, pours
himself a drink, swallows it down, does the same again,
then rests his head on the desk and beats the desk
with his glass)

JANET. December 3rd. Dear sir ... No ... Dear Mr.
    Kooning ... No ... Alec ... I've been ill, desperately
    ill, people said I would die and it's all your fault. I

116

wrote to you and I said I'd read all of your books and
I meant it, though I haven't managed to read them
all yet. Anyway, they're hard to get hold of, you've
got to go poking around in all sorts of places to find
them and the lady behind the counter gave me a very
hard look when I asked for them, a very hard look, as
much to say, well, she said she didn't remember there
being any such books, which is a lie, I think. Anyway,
I did read some of them, and I did write to you, you
beast, and you never answered ... and I've been ill
and I could've died were it not for that old cow of a
mother of mine who officiously saved my life by
making me sick up a whole two bottles of soluble
aspirin ... ugh ... I dreamed about you, Alec, you
were very tall, greying at the temples, of course,
slim, slightly bent, bowed, I mean, at the shoulders,
what they call a scholar's stoop and looking very very
wise, like a snowy old owl but even more beautiful,
and I climbed on your back and you spread your
enormous feathery wings and we flew high into the
clouds and you told me that I was the first person
you'd ever given a ride to and ... no ... no ....
you're not like a snowy owl; on the contrary, you're
a nasty, selfish old crow who won't write letters ...
you're a ... no ... Dear Mr. Kooning, The fact that
you didn't reply to my letter implies, I suppose ...
no ...
Dear Mr. Kooning, I hope you won't mind me writing
to you again. Please put this letter straight into the
waste-paper basket if I'm being a nuisance. The fact
is (to be quite honest) I was not really telling the whole
truth when I said I'd managed to read all your books.
Try as I might I can't get hold of "The Last Cry" and
I wonder if you know how I can get hold of a copy. If
all this is a bore for you I apologise and sign myself a
fan who is also a bother. Janet Rosenberg.

JANET. Dec. 5th. Dear Mr. Kooning, What a surprise
after all my glum surmising. This morning, I was
just washing my hair, doing all those ridiculous things
that girls have to do to prepare themselves "to meet
the faces that we meet" as old Tom Eliot would put
it, when lo and behold, a ring at the front door, me
rushing down, hair all wet and soapy, a towel wrapped

117

round it and standing at the door, who do you think?
the Postmaster General, no less, surely not a mere
postman anyway, in gold braid and in his hand, ~~ias~~
as if it were nothing at all, a big, big parcel. And
that's not all, because standing beside the Postmaster
General was a lady from Inter-Flora with a huge,
huge, enormous bundle of roses. I tore upstairs,
leaving little puddles of hair-water in my wake, for-
getting all about the crown of soap suds and all fingers
and thumbs tore at the parcel like a savage wild cat,
all silver claws, and revealed, well, thank-you,
thank-you, dear, good, kind Mr. Kooning, Alec, I
suppose I should call you now since that's how you
signed yourself in all those lovely, crisp, uncut
copies of your works, from A to Z, all signed and for
me. And the roses, the roses, the room is filled
with the roses and the rumour of your voice, dear
good Mr. Kooning - so many thank-you's I can't write
them out. I shall begin at the beginning, the very first,
I shall cut the pages so carefully, scissors like silver
butterflies they'll be, and read and read and read. And
I shall read the roses too. What do they say, I wonder,
what message is printed in scarlet on their stalks?
Yours faithfully, Janet (Rosenberg).

ALEC. Dec. 10th. Dear Janet (Rosenberg), I don't understand it at all. Days I've sat here in my candle-lit
chamber, never going out, drinking bottles of whiskey
and getting more and more bemused. At my time of
life, at my age, sear and yellow and what not, it's
not nice to get nasty shocks, rather awful as a matter
of fact and the matter of fact that I'm talking about,
here is a fog of drink and cigars, is this - are you
having me on - roses, you say, what bloody rose, I
hate roses, great red petulant things, did I send roses,
I think not, and yet, and yet ... Being gaga starts
North of 65, that's my hypothesis, unless these
spasms and pains in my joints and the head-aches and
the way my heart suddenly jumps and then races, all
means, of God, that I'm suffering from the thinkers'
disease, arterio-sclerosis, from which Yeats died,,
but he was old, not sprightly, in the spring of old
age, not fifty, for God's sake. Are you having me on,
or did I, in an aberrant moment, pick up the phone

and send those roses. And another thing, oh, my
head, those books you mentioned, those uncut books,
how could I, I've been remaindered for years, I think
I have, and another thing, another thing, the titles,
so many books; you've got it all wrong, young woman,
you're crazy, you're writing to the wrong man, I tell
you, or you're writing to everybody and ... and ... or
you're having me on ... all those titles, weirdly
like the few books I wrote so many summers past,
weirdly like the thought of books I wrote in my head ... I
don't understand, I don't understand, my head is
aching, my breath smells and I'm not feeling well ...
reply at once and in haste ... what am I saying ... ?
Alec.

ALEC. Dec. 15th. Dear Janet, You do not reply and I
think I am going out of my mind ... I sit here and
stare into space and then, out of a mist, I begin to
see you ... (He swivels in his chair - stares at JANET
who stares at him) Your face forms in the air and
you smile, grin rather, and I reach out to touch you
and I can't ... my paws paw the air ... Janet, say
something, write, and a line of poetry keeps on
going round and round in my head ...

JANET. 'Now all day long the noise of battle rolled ...'

ALEC. Yes, that one and, 'They flee from me that sometime
did me seek'.

JANET. 'With naked foot stalking in my chamber'.

(JANET gets up, crosses into ALEC's room)

ALEC. I've seen them gentle tame and meek

JANET. That sometime put themselves in danger

ALEC. To take bread at my hand

JANET. But now all's changed ...

ALEC. Into a bitter fashion of forsaking ...

119

JANET. This is your room, then, Alec ... ?

ALEC. Yes, yes, this is my room.

JANET. This is where all the famous words are written ...

ALEC. I suppose so ...

JANET. It's very untidy ...

ALEC. Oh, I dunno ...

JANET. It is ... it is ... very untidy.

ALEC. Why did you write to me?

JANET. I don't know.

ALEC. A whim, was it?

JANET. I don't know.

ALEC. You must know.

JANET. Well, I don't. Is this an original manuscript?

ALEC. What ... no ... leave that alone ...

JANET. It's a letter.

ALEC. Put it down.

JANET. It's addressed to me.

ALEC. Put it down.

JANET. No. It's my letter. It's not your letter. When you write letters to people they become the letters of the people you write to.

ALEC. Rubbish. Leave it alone.

JANET. They become the property of the people whose name is inscribed on the envelope.

ALEC. Not till they're posted, they don't.

JANET. The moment they're written.

ALEC. I absolutely forbid you to open that letter.

JANET. Why?

ALEC. Give it to me.

JANET. Why?

ALEC. Never mind why.

JANET. Shan't.

ALEC. Shall.

JANET. Shan't.

ALEC. Shall. Bloody shall.

JANET. Bloody shan't.

ALEC. Give me that bloody letter or it'll be the worse
for you.

JANET. Not till you tell me what's in it.

ALEC. No.

JANET. All right. I'll read it ...

ALEC. I'll kill you if you read that letter.

JANET. Pooh.

ALEC. I will. I'll kill you.

(He pursues her. They grapple ...)

JANET. Alec. Alec. You're hurting me.

ALEC. Will ... you ... give me that letter ...

JANET. No. No. Never. Not while there's one drop of
air in my body ...

ALEC. I'll ... I'll ... oh ... all right ... I'll tell you
what's in it ...

JANET. Good boy.

ALEC. It's nothing really.

JANET. Liar.

ALEC. Nothing, I tell you ... well ... all it says is ...

JANET. This had better be good ...

ALEC. (cunningly) Actually, I've forgotten what's in it.
You'll have to give it back to me so's I can read it
out to you.

JANET. Foxy.

ALEC. Scout's honour.

JANET. Cross your heart and hope to die.

ALEC. Yes.

JANET. Do it then.

ALEC. There. (Does it) Now can I have that letter?

JANET. Mmmmm. All right. (Gives it to him) I trust
you, mind.

ALEC. More fool you. (He tears it up into pieces) There,
now you'll never know what's in it.

JANET. Beast. Rotten, horrible, silly beast. I hope you
do die. I don't admire you any more. You're just a
silly, rotten, horrible beast and I hope the guns get
you.

ALEC. Yah.

JANET. I hope you get blown up ... I hope you hang with your guts all trailing over the wire, I hope you get horribly mutilated ... I hope ...

ALEC. I'll tell you what was in it, if you like ...

JANET. Shut up.

ALEC. It was ...

JANET. Shut up ...

ALEC. It was a love letter.

JANET. Oh?

ALEC. Yes. Rather embarrassing actually ... full of sentimental slop it was really, all about your twinkling eyes and cherry lips and downy bosom ...

JANET. Downy bosom, eh?

ALEC. And so on, in technicolour prose, right down to your ankles ...

JANET. Is that true?

ALEC. Scout's ...

JANET. Liar.

ALEC. Well, it was a sort of a love letter. Listen and I'll tell you what it said.

JANET. Truth, mind.

ALEC. Yes. Come on. Sit down. Make yourself comfortable. Put your curly bonce on my knee-caps and listen to the story.

JANET. Yes, Daddy.

ALEC. Well, beauty, once upon a time ...

JANET. Mmmmm.

ALEC. There was this fabulously successful writer ...

JANET. Autobiographical, is it?

ALEC. Shhhhh ... fabulously successful writer and one day
he was sitting in the room where he'd written all his
fabulously successful works and he was brooking ...
yes ... brooding he was and as he brooded and his
great big brain turned over one huge thought after
another, he noticed ... what d'you think?

JANET. Mmmm?

ALEC. I said 'what do you think he noticed?'

JANET. Dunno.

ALEC. Well, what he noticed, peeping around the corner
of one of the many gilt-edged volumes of his gilt-edged
works was the small pink nose of a mouse ...

JANET. Really ...

ALEC. Yeah. A mouse, honest.

JANET. Hmmmm.

ALEC. A little furry grey field-mouse, strayed in from
the fields, no doubt, the fecund acres of his wide
ranging establishment ... Quick as a flash ...

JANET. Is this a nice story?

ALEC. Yes, shut up ... quick as a flash his hand snapped
out and there was the mouse struggling and squeaking
between his fingers.

JANET. It's not a ...

ALEC. Shut up ...

JANET. I don't ...

124

ALEC. Ah, sighed he, this fabulous writer, and he squeezed the mouse between his fingers ...

JANET. Yeeeuuh ... (Puts her fingers over her ears)

ALEC. Such a squeal, you never did hear the like ...
(He pulls her hands away and whispers into her ear)
and he crushed and he crushed did the awful giant, and
the mouses squealed and squealed and he shrieked at
the mouse, that's for all the humiliations you've
inflicted on me, that's for death and the pain you've
given me, that's for the gift of a life of terror and loneliness, that's for the last horror when your lungs
are in your mouth, and the blood comes down through
your nose.

(JANET gets up, backs away in her own room; the
lights dim on her side)

... that's for the girls that lay down in every direction and never a one for me, that's for their laughs and
their giggles and their stupid stupid little sneering
faces, that's for all of it, humiliation, torture, defeat,
loneliness, pain, sickness, all of it, all of it, and
the mouse squealed and squealed and his squeal is
still rising to the height of the stars and I took him
and with all the strength in my body I flung him as
far as I could. And then do you know what happened ...
do you? Do you ... ?

(He stares ahead. At nothing. Continues)

Well, it was rather extraodrinary, really, because
as this mouse was flying through the air, suddenly
there was a flash in the sky and a burst of music and
Mighty Mouse came roaring down from a cloud, caught
this little terrified mouse in his great muscular paws,
carried him up aloft, all the time administering magic
mouse nostrums that had this mouse fit as a fiddle
in a trice and the last I saw all the cats were defeated
and lost their teeth into the bargain and everybody
suddenly burst out singing, the lights went up and
everybody lived happily ever after.

(He looks up, swivels in his chair. Picks up his pen, begins to write)

Dear Mouse, A most extraordinary thing happened. Like a vision, really. I suppose I've been overworking or something, stress, something like that, but really, it was so extraordinary ... listen, my dear, I must see you, I must _actually_ see you. Please write and tell me it'll be all right if I come to see you. It's important to me. Love, Alec.

JANET. Dear Alec, If you must, you must, but really I think it better if you do not. I don't know why, it's a feeling I have, that this kindness of yours in replying to my silly adoring letters and the silly way I write, just anything, really, that comes into my head, it's all been spoiled ... we'd not be the same, I'm not clever to tell you what I'm trying to say, Alec, but wouldn't it be nice just to write those strange, mysterious letters to each other and one sad day when you were dead and all the important people were jostling around your grave I'd be on the periphery, a sad, forlorn, young lady, dressed in gay colours, but forlorn and they'd say, 'Who's that?', 'The love of his life', they'd say, faithful for years, just like D. H. Lawrence and Miss Burroughs that came to his graveside in Vence, it'd be sad, Alec, but so beautiful. Don't come to see me. Please. Don't come to see me.

Scene Two

(ALEC and MRS ROSENBERG in JANET's room. They are sitting silently, uncomfortably, waiting for something to say)

ALEC. Yes ... er ... I'm a writer. I write ... novels, mainly. (Pause) Yes. (Recklessly) Of course, there are other literary forms, epic, lyric, tragic, comic ... other genres ... tried my hand at all of them ... yes ... but, when the chips are down it's the novel that gets my vote, the art of Austen, Trollope, if you'll pardon the expression, Conrad, Foster, Virginia Woolf, James ... Joyce and others too numerous to mention ... Dostoievsky, for instance, ... The Idiot and Tolstoy ... great spirits, those, imaginations in the upper-imagery bracket ... don't you think so?

MRS ROSENBERG. I've always admired Annie Besant myself.

ALEC. Really ... novelist of genius, was she?

MRS ROSENBERG. Well ... em ... actually, she was more on the religious side, I think.

ALEC. Woman of God, eh?

MRS ROSENBERG. I don't really know.

ALEC. Ah. (Pause) Janet ...

MRS ROSENBERG. She used to have visions, I believe.

ALEC. Janet did?

MRS ROSENBERG. Towards the beginning of the century.

ALEC. Oh, yes. Well....

MRS ROSENBERG. You'd prefer to wait, wouldn't you?

ALEC. Er ... yes ... yes ... I suppose so ...

MRS. ROSENBERG. (rising) I'll leave you to it, then.

ALEC. Thank-you.

MRS ROSENBERG. (goes to the door) Of course, nobody ever consults me.

ALEC. Oh?

MRS ROSENBERG. Nobody ever says 'May I do this, Mother?' 'May I do that?' They don't you know.

ALEC. It's ... er ... infuriating, I agree.

MRS ROSENBERG. You bear them and what thanks do you get?

ALEC. I know what you mean.

MRS ROSENBERG. I wonder if you do, Mr ... er ...

ALEC. Kooning.

MRS ROSENBERG. You've never been a woman, have you?

ALEC. Well, if I have, I've had a lot of funny experiences.

MRS ROSENBERG. It's no joke, Mr. Kooning.

ALEC. No ... no.

MRS ROSENBERG. You bear them in your womb, you lose your figure, you get varicose veins, you suffer terrible agony, you feed them; I breast-fed all mine, Mr. Kooning ...

ALEC. Really!

MRS ROSENBERG. Yes. Every one. My nipples used to be raw.

ALEC. I didn't know that.

MRS ROSENBERG. How could you?

ALEC. Well ... I ... er ...

MRS ROSENBERG. Raw ... often I used to think, if that baby chews much harder it'll be feeding on blood ...

ALEC. God almighty. I thought it was supposed to be a pleasure.

MRS. ROSENBERG. (sits down. Puts her hand on his knee) Pleasure! Pleasure! Did you say 'pleasure'?

ALEC. Well, I only thought ... I ... isn't it, then?

MRS ROSENBERG. It's agony. From beginning to end.

ALEC. Why didn't you bottle-feed them, then?

MRS ROSENBERG. What?

ALEC. Why didn't you feed them on the bottle?

MRS ROSENBERG. I'm sorry ... ?

ALEC. I was saying, if it was agony ...

MRS ROSENBERG. Agony, yes, you've got no idea ...

ALEC. Well, what I was asking was ...

MRS ROSENBERG. Would you, Mr. Kooning, take a careful look at me.

ALEC. Er ... certainly ...

MRS ROSENBERG. A thorough examination, mind you.

ALEC. How d'you mean?

MRS ROSENBERG. Right. Now. Just take a good look.

(ALEC looks. She turns round in front of him)

As a man, would you say I was still attractive ... as a woman, I mean ...

ALEC. Very, yes.

MRS ROSENBERG. Really?

ALEC. Yes. You're a very attractive woman.

MRS ROSENBERG. Would you say I was ... what's the word ... desirable?

ALEC. Definitely.

MRS ROSENBERG. Would you like to make love ... to me, then?

ALEC. What now?

MRS ROSENBERG. If you want to, yes.

ALEC. Here, in Janet's room?

MRS ROSENBERG. It's not Janet's room. It's my room.

ALEC. Oh ... your room, is it?

MRS ROSENBERG. Yes. It's my room.

ALEC. Well, Mrs. Rosenberg, it was Janet I came to see, actually ... I ...

MRS.ROSENBERG. I see ...

ALEC. (lamely) We've been corresponding, you see ... (Pause) ... so ... it wouldn't be right ... don't you think ... it wouldn't be ethical .

MRS ROSENBER. Mr. Kooning ...

ALEC. Not ... in view of the ... er ... circumstances ...

MRS ROSENBERG. ... how we're placed ...

ALEC. Exactly. Henry Miller might've managed it ... in his heyday ... but me ... I'm not that sort of writer ... more pastoral than passionate ... more ... how shall I say ... homogeneous than heterogeneous ...

(He is acutely embarrassed, tugs hopelessly at his tie)

MRS ROSENBERG. My situation is not fortunate ...

ALEC. I've always tried to ... to ... you get these bouts and spasms and then you're off ... but I've always tried to ...

130

MRS ROSENBERG. ... it took a lot out of me to say what
        I said to you ...

ALEC. ... and sometimes ... I'm sorry, what did
        you say?

MRS ROSENBERG. Inside one doesn't change at all ...
        only when one takes a look in the mirror one sees the
        face of a stranger, an old raddled stranger.

ALEC. Oh, but you're ...

MRS ROSENBERG. Your stockings get wrinkled, for no
        good reason at all that I can see ... instead of staying
        up ... you see disgust ...

ALEC. In your prime ... really ...

MRS ROSENBERG. ... where formerly interest was ...

ALEC. No, no.

MRS ROSENBERG. But I thought ... I thought ... an older
        man ... somebody ... like yourself ...

ALEC. Mmm, I see ...

MRS ROSENBERG. But you came to see Janet ...

ALEC.. Yes, I was saying ... she wrote to me, I wrote to
        her ... ahem ... perfectly natural, innocent ...

MRS ROSENBERG. I'll leave you then ... (She stays put)

ALEC. Though why one does ... God knows ...

MRS ROSENBERG. Sometimes one feels like a bird trapped
        in a coal-mine, flying for miles and miles of black
        stone corridors, never a sign of light, just darker
        and darker, and at the end ...

ALEC. Splash.

MRS ROSENBERG. What?

131

ALEC. At the end, splash ...

MRS ROSENBERG. Yes.

ALEC. (passionately) I know what you mean. I know what you mean. But we've got a few tricks left up our sleeves yet eh ... a few tricks ...

MRS ROSENBERG. Splash. Very true. Very true.

ALEC. My feet sweat, my tongue's coloured like a charcoal biscuit but inside, what! Inside, Mrs. Rosenberg, resilience, hope ... inside ...

MRS ROSENBERG. So I thought to myself, why not; why not say it straight out, so I did.

ALEC. Yes.

MRS ROSENBERG. Yes.

ALEC. Yes.

MRS ROSENBERG. Well ...

ALEC. Indeed.

MRS ROSENBERG. It's odd, isn't it?

ALEC. Yes.

MRS ROSENBERG. Odd.

ALEC. Yes.

MRS ROSENBERG. People of our age, you'd think, wouldn't you, we'd have so much to talk about, there'd be so much less, the walls'd be so much thinner, between us ... people our age, so much more interesting, so much more dipped and dyed in experience, don't you think, so much to say ...

ALEC. Direct contact with the soul of the language ... or the other way round ...

132

MRS ROSENBERG. But it's not true ...

ALEC. Alas!

MRS ROSENBERG. We cannot, Mr. Kooning, share, any
    longer, the illusion of being able to help each other.

ALEC. Far too well aware of being in the full blast of the
    er ... metaphysical tragedy of the species ... that's
    our trouble.

MRS ROSENBERG. So ...

ALEC. ... as a famous writer once wrote ...

MRS ROSENBERG. ... that being the case ...

ALEC. ... to me personally ...

MRS ROSENBERG. I'll leave you, then ...

ALEC. ... in a letter he was writing to posterity ...

MRS ROSENBERG. I said, I'll leave you then ...

ALEC. The bastard!

MRS ROSENBERG. I said ...

ALEC. Oh, yes, I'm sorry ... thank-you ... er ...

MRS ROSENBERG. Not at all. (She goes to the door) You
    know, Mr. Kooning ...

ALEC. Yes?

MRS ROSENBERG. The reason I didn't use a bottle ...

ALEC. Eh?

MRS ROSENBERG. The reason was, I think I can say this
    in all sincerity ... was ...

ALEC. Yes ...

MRS ROSENBERG. It was during the war, after all ...

ALEC. Was it?

MRS ROSENBERG. During the blitz ... they were flinging everything at us.

ALEC. Yes, I remember ...

MRS ROSENBERG. Incendiaries, V bombs, crunch, crunch, crunch ... we were all down in the shelters ... we used to listen to Winnie's broadcasts in the shelters ...

ALEC. We will fight them in the back-alleys, we will fight them ...

MRS ROSENBERG. A very gifted man, an inspired leader.

ALEC. Yes.

MRS ROSENBERG. Well, I thought, raw breasts or no, if German women can feed their children on the breast and not on the bottle, it's up to us to show those Germans we're just as good as they are, better if it comes to that ...

ALEC. There's always been an England ...

MRS ROSENBERG. And England shall be free ...

ALEC. If England does as much to you ...

MRS ROSENBERG. I'll bring you a cup of tea ...

(Exits)

ALEC. That's not the last line. Jesus Christ. I've always wanted life, as in art, to be irritatingly obvious, but in my case it keeps on going askew. Loony old bag, milk's probably gone to her head. Janet ... (Shouts) Janet ... !

ACT TWO

Scene One

(Same scene. ALEC trying to remember the first line
of "There'll always be an England".

ALEC. (to himself) "There's always been an England" ...
I think that's where we went wrong ... (Sings) 'There's
always been an England , And England shall be free,
If England does as much to you ... er ... If England
does as much to you (Roars out triumphantly) I'll
bring you a cup of tea'. She hasn't though. Vanished
without trace ... not even a smear of lipstick, grease
of a thumbprint to show she's even been ... it's
always like that ... few bones in a box, that's it ...
mustn't be morbid. Huh! (Surveys the room) The
rooms of young females are always the same ...
(Pause) Half on virginity, half on the game. Yes.
Ha, ha. Janet? An invisible girl from Traquair
complained that she'd nothing to wear, she said,
though Nosey Parkers can't see that I'm starkers
they can feel with their hands that I'm bare.

(A stifled giggle. ALEC looks curious)

Janet. You there, Janet? (Shouts) Janet ...

JANET. Date. January 16th. Dear Alec ...

ALEC. Janet?

JANET. Shhh ... Dear Alec, I told you not to come, but

135

you would come ...

ALEC. Where are you?

JANET. ... and now see what's happened.

ALEC. Come out and show yourself ...

(Silence)

Janet ... where are you. Oh, come on, eh? (Starts
to look around) Come on. It's infra dig poking around
in a young girl's bedroom. Janet ... puss, puss. All
right. I'll just sit here, till you decide to stop being
childish. Okay? Right. (Pause) Your mother is a
fruit and nut-case. Did you hear her ... going on ... ?
Jesus ... ! She practically had me stripped down and up
to me elbows in geriatric intercourse. Incredible.
(Pause) Don't you think? Strange. Funny behaviour.
Bizarre. Peculiar. Not normal - wouldn't you say,
Janet? A bit stark-raving disgusting bonkers. Still,
I sympathise really. I say I sympathise. Poor old
sod, sits here all day twitching away at the curtains
and sees you every morning, ripening, all peach
blossom and succulent goodness - 'nuff to drive you
round the bend. Would me. Would me, I say, Sod it.
Where are you. Eh. Janet. Oh, all right. (Sighs)
Date. Jan. 16th. My dear Janet, Where are you?
I've called at your house today and was greeted by
Lady Macbeth who tried to get me to stab here with my
invisible dagger. But I did not. Yours faithfully,
Alec Kooning.

JANET. Dear Alec, Be serious. I told you about my awful
old mum. And I told you what it would be like. Ah, well.
Never mind. You came, and that's all that matters.
Love Janet.

ALEC. Dear Janet, I'm glad you think so. Love, Alec.

JANET. Dearest Alec, I mean it. It was lovely to see you.
On the other hand ...

ALEC. Dear Janet, What? Alec.

JANET. Dear Famous Alec, ... on the other hand, you're
not at all what I expected. You're ... what shall I
say ... plump ... fat even ... actually, you're rather
gross ...

ALEC. Dearest Janet, Thanks very much.

JANET. Rather like a red pudding, in fact, though your
hair is grey and you've got a kind face.

ALEC. I want to see you ...

(Silence)

I've come all this way and I want to see your face.
I do. I've got such a palpable image in my mind,
Janet. So palpable, I feel, if I put my fingers through
my eyes I'll be able to touch your face, it's so clear
to me ... Please, Janet, wherever you are, please
come out. Please. Listen, to be quite honest, I don't
understand, and I don't like this funny idea you've
got of only speaking as if you were writing a letter,
there's something, I don't know ... horrible about
it ... I don't know ... gory even, dear Janet ...

JANET. Dear Alec, Yes?

ALEC. ... come on, eh? Just a bloody glimpse ...

JANET. Dear Alec, It was funny, wasn't it ...

ALEC. Aaaaaaaaa!

JANET. ... there you were, as large as life, twice as
irritated, sitting on my bed and I wouldn't talk to you
and you sat there saying all sorts of weird things and
finally I said something and you started to try to get
me to join you and I protested but you looked so pathetic, Alec, sitting there, all huffed because I'd said
you were fat and feeling, I'm sure, a bit nonplussed
that I began to feel quite sorry for you, lo how are the
mighty fallen, I did warn you, tthough, didn't I, and
finally I felt really tempted to come out ...

ALEC. Yes ... hey, why are you ... ?

JANET. But I wouldn't and then I laughed ... (She laughs) and you got angry ...

ALEC. (angrily) I did not ... I mean, I am not.

JANET. ... Anyway, there you were, all forlorn and indignant, and me watching you, feeling more and more tempted to come out ...

ALEC. (suddenly gets the idea. Says cunningly) And there I was, dear Janet, sitting on your bed, lusting for a sight of you and you were being all silly and coy but finally you did come out ... ah ...

(JANET steps out from behind some curtain or round the door)

ALEC. I'm beginning to get the hang of this. Yes, you did, framed in the golden light, like a beautiful, young, innocent vision ...

JANET. And finally I took pity on you and I came out.

ALEC. You stood there and I rose and went towards you and I took you in my arms and I kissed you, I kissed the nape of your swan neck, the tips of your ears, and so on, and drew you slowly, inexorably, towards the bed, and although you protested ...

JANET. I said 'Hello, Alec' and for a moment there seemed nothing more to say and then I motioned you to a seat and we began a long discussion on some aspects of the modern novel ...

ALEC. You started to say something about the art of Iris Murdoch ...

JANET. 'Don't you think' I said ...

ALEC. But overcome by your terrible innocence, by your need, Janet, your vulnerability.

JANET. ... What's so curious about her novels ...

ALEC. I stopped your voice with kisses, lifted you up
       and ... staggered ... towards the bed ...

JANET. Dear Alec ...

ALEC. 'Shut up' I said, not irritably, but in that brusque,
       lovable way some men have ... we ... collapsed ...
       blast ... and I hurt myself on the bloody bed-post ...
       ouch ... ooooh ...

JANET. Then you hurt yourself, rather badly, I'm afraid ...

ALEC. (Begins to pull up his trouser-leg) Eh?

JANET. (firmly) ... rather badly - 'Oh, you poor thing ...

ALEC. Bloody hell ... ow ...

JANET. I cried 'you poor, poor thing' and I assisted you,
        still groaning loudly and protesting, poor darling.

ALEC. ow, ow, ow.

JANET. ... to the bed ...

ALEC. Oh?

JANET. ... and just to make sure the damage wasn't too
        bad I started to undress you ...

ALEC. You did? Yes, you did. I lay there like a stone,
       very badly ... no, not very badly damaged but
       suffering quite a bit ... ow, ow, though, under your
       cool fingers, ouch, your cool, but rather careless
       fingers, the agony began to quickly abate somewhat -
       you heaved off ... oooooh ... drew off my trousers
       and ...

JANET. ... and then I remembered where I was ...

ALEC. ... but your compassion overcame your sense of
       propriety, you took off my shoes first because, idiot!

hope + fantasy.

139

Little idiot that you are, you thought you could tear
off my trousers without first removing my shoes, ah,
lovely ... then my socks ... he hum, and finally
off came my trousers and the livid but, as it turned
out, harmless weal on my leg was revealed.

JANET. Goodness, I cried, it's bad, really bad ... and I
tried to staunch the blood.

ALEC. Blood! Blood! ... but your eyes were deceiving
you, because there was no blood, not a speck, not
a bloody speck, just this very impressive, livid weal ...

JANET. Oh, I said, oh, this calls for medical attention.
I've seen such weals, I said, when I was once in a
hospital, first signs, the doctors used to say, first
signs of a gangrenous ligature ...

ALEC. Thank God, I cried, after you had showed me the full
depths of your medical ignorance, thank God it's not
worse - oh, Janet, I exclaimed, stroke my brows
with your tiny finger-tips and you did, by God, you
did, you came right on to the bed and out of your
compassion and more than compassion, a kind of
overpowering love, you came, lay down beside me,
murmuring ...

JANET. I thought you'd lost consciousness so I leant over
to catch your breathing ...

ALEC. Suddenly my arms flew round you like a steel
trap; Janet, I cried, this thing is too strong for both
of us, slowly, slowly, the blood mounted, we kissed
... kissed, I say ... kissed.

JANET. Mmmmm ... I gave you the kiss of life ...

ALEC. Huh ... and kissed for dear life again ... Janet,
Janet, I murmured, I want you, Janet, I want you.

JANET. But you never managed to tell me what you wanted
because suddenly you were doubled up with a violent
pain in your stomach ...

140

(She knees him)

ALEC. Ow ... oooooh ... but my stomach muscles were
like iron and so was all the rest of me, I took you in
my arms again and said ...

JANET. (desperately) I ... April 16th ... April 19th ...
(Or whatever date fits in with the first date)

ALEC. Not a word more, I said, or it'll be the death of
you, death, death, death, and you became still and
docile. I swear, God forgive me, if you'd not succumbed
at that moment, I'd have strangled you, raped you,
murdered you there and then, but you saw the danger
signals and anyway you loved me with all your heart and
I began those beautiful preliminaries, so long remembered, almost forgotten ... (Stares at her. A long
pause. A change of tone) ... almost forgotten ... The
anxieties, the embarrassments, the sheer silliness
of the whole comical enterprise, your silent, wounded
face, my dear, your humanity, and suddenly, alas,
I felt old and sad, (I can't make love in the past tense
and love seems to be all in the past tense for me
nowadays) and I got up, not without regret and a touch
of longing ...

JANET. I called you back and I said 'Yes, I will, if you
want me'; and you did come back, Alec, you did and
you weren't defeated ...

ALEC. I came back and stood looking down at you and I
said 'I'm sorry, my love, very sorry and I am,
Janet, I am, very sorry, and I took my coat and I
took my hat and walked, trying to keep together the
remnants of my dignity, walked slowly, so slowly,
to the door and the world outside ...

JANET. And if I'd not said, timidly, Alec, you've forgotten your trousers, you old fool, you'd have gone
off, into the world, with a sad look on your silly,
old face, a hat on, a coat on, in your underpants and
with no socks and shoes ... God, Alec, you are a
fool ...

Scene Two

(ALEC, back in his room, darkness on JANET's
side, ALEC bleary, the worse for much drink, but
speaking clearly, in full possession, etc.)

ALEC. May 28th. Dear Janet, It's midnight. Time for
owls and wombats, marsupials of all sorts to come
slurping across the carpet ... for the tapers of my
soul to drip darkness into the teapots of time ...
not drunk, Janet, only enormously sober ... all day
slavering over a stiff whisky ... why'd ye never
write no more ... there's cobwebs on the letter-box
... no more ... today, yesterday, the day before
that, they've all passed like a flash, a grey flash ...
I've cleaned out my nose, been to the lavatory and
back fourteen times, all without issue ... God knows
what it's like inside, standing room only but ... but
... dear Janet ... I feel I'm on the verge of a break-
down ... no ... fool ... funny thing that ... I feel,
Janet, I'm on the verge of a breakthrough, a breakthrough, I think I've found the answer to the secret
of life, but I'm keeping it to myself. Though between
you and me and the thing that keeps slurping across
my carpet ... Gerroff ... Listen, Janet, if you'll
keep it to yourself, I'll let you into the secret, which
is, by and large, taking everything into account, that
'can' and 'ought' have the same meaning, what a
tedious semantic mind I've got ... no, listen, Janet,
before this gigantic, hairy marsupial pops me into her
furry basket, the secret is 'Virtue comes with practise' ... ha, ha, ha ... listen, Janet, now listen,
when you get this letter, pop it straight down into
your bosom ,.. Christ, listen, I'm trying to tell you,
you wrote to me, to me, you bloody intruder, so
despite everything, your need is greater than mine,
much, much greater ... so that's why I'll never let
go of you, never, I'll rage under your bedclothes, I'll
ride rough-shod over your eiderdown, I'm in marvellous condition, I'll fill your belly with hairy marsupials, they're the coming species, the days of the

inside womb are numbered so, though, to you I may
appear grey, red-eared, with enormously powerful
sweat-glands working night and day to generate an
overpowering stench of decay, though you despise age,
though the old might just as well be dead as living,
though I slurp me soup, I do, I know that, I have
shirts stiff with soup hanging up in the wardrobe, shirts
hardly worn, stiff with soup and garlanded with spag-
hetti ... granting these truths, Janet, still, still,
Janet, I cut myself and cross this letter with red
kisses, sign myself your ancient, tried and true,
marsupial lover ... in potentia ... in potentia ...
Alec.

(Darkness a second or so. Lights up to ALEC, more
ravaged than ever)

(The voice of JANET, pensive, in the middle of a
letter to ALEC)

JANET. But it's so sad, isn't it, when it's pouring with
rain and the wind blows and the poor flowers are
nodding their heads ... never mind ... never mind ...
I have my own garden of ideas, Alec, and it grows ...
strangely enough I had a casual encounter the other
day and he expressed an interest in this novel I've
been writing, you remember, I'm sure I told you,
anyway, what with one thing and another, it's good
news, exciting really, but I'm trying to keep calm
... my urge is to go out and buy and buy and buy ...
but I won't ... I don't think I will. Alec, I'm so grate-
ful to you. The past, the present and the future have
note, touched and parted in us. Always, always I will
remember you and your kindness. I shall never forget.
Best wishes. Janet Rosenberg, Author.

ALEC. Jesus Christ, woman, your last letter was abominable, tore open the envelope, read your abominable
letter, abominable letter, don't want to hear all that
bloody trivia, ignorant, twisted, childish bloody
nonsense ... 'went out shopping, met this ignorant,
infant yahoo, chatted all night, such intelligence,
writing a novel, publisher amazed ...' 'Course he's
bloody amazed, anybody would be, wrap your legs

round his abdomen he'll publish anything, me, me, me,
what about me, nonsense, that's what you write,
fatuous rubbish, hateful, bloody, pygmy sentences, let
me tell you, sentences, Janet, need time to grow, need
time, had sentences growing in me since I was twelve
some of them nine yards long still growing still
incubating keep them there deprived of full stops till
the day they're ready giants giant sentences ...
(This all in a rush, takes a huge break) but, no, you'll
be up the stick to the first hairless, pink-eyed organ
winks at you ... trivial, futile, listen, last night, in
bed, lying there, not thinking, had this terrible sensation in the pit of my stomach, cancer, I thought, it's
got me, cancer, but no, Janet, no, it was not cancer,
it was not cancer, on the contrary, it was a sign of
health, vigour, a sign of hope. Write to me as you
did. Write to me. Tell me good things. Alec.

(Darkness again. Then light on ALEC, very far gone
in desperation)

ALEC. (in a hoarse whisper) Baa, baa, black sheep, have
you any wool? No, I flaming haven't. I'm all out of
bloody wool. I've been fleeced by an expert. Dis-
covered, this morning, seven more veins in my nose.
I wrote that down. Tally now stands at 47. Is this a
record? Also find that if I leave a cigar-butt to stand
for 48 hours and then inhale it, I can still get a slight
sensation of pleasure - nothing spectacular, but it
shows the lungs are still in full working order, in a
sound condition. I have fantasies of writing a very
funny book, all cryptic, full of very minute sentences,
I have visions that if I can get this book hard-printed
and distributed, over a wide area, in no time at all
everybody'll be so organised that every-time their
mouths try to utter a black thought or a monstrous
lie, nothing'll happen ... it'll all be the way Karl
Marx said it'd be in the nations of mankind. Once
went there, Janet, went on a pilgrimage, took a
tube to Highgate Station, walked bloody miles in the
grilling sunshine, wanted, Christ knows what I
wanted, to kow-tow to a huge statue, got there,
bloody fiasco, the gates were all shut, two hundred
yards from those mighty bones, Janet ... two hundred

yards. Cover my grave with kisses, I died old.
Yours faithfully, A. Kooning.

Scene Three

JANET. (writes, pad on knee, for herself) I'm bored with
him, fed up to the back teeth, time I was finished
with him, that old incubus, hanging around my neck,
an old clapped out Albatross, nothing but hard luck,
time to have done with him, write him out of my life
... he represents, I see that now, everything that
is obscene, sentimental, self-indulgent, undisting-
uished, gross, material, nasty, decadent, unvigorous,
everything bad ... in things ... look at him now, how
ridiculous he is, puffing and panting, heart condition,
I shouldn't wonder, a life of constant self-flagellation,
in one form or another, a bundle of anxieties, looking
desperately for a banana skin, huh, what a fiasco,
his heavy old torso collapsed and gasping over her
trim body. I can see him, even now, suspended
between one mechanical reflex and another ... (She
looks up at ALEC) ... What a creation!

ALEC. She keeps on saying I'm an old man, she reiterates
that thesis; I've aged certainly, a mile in four minutes is just not within the bounds of possibility, but
I'm still with it, constantly with it. I must just keep
going ...

JANET. Poor broken, old man ... When the will to live
begins to break ...

ALEC. Ever since she came into my life, my life has
been at sixes and sevens, if that's the right number
... and now she's taken to writing ... sucks the
pap from my mouth ... after that fiasco, which was
no fault of mine ... must just keep going, must just
bear the load ...

JANET. He keeps on writing these letters, these crazy
letters, all covered over with red x's, saying he's
rejuvenated ... but I'm writing him out of my life ...
I'm ...

145

ALEC. My Dear Janet, Woke up this morning, fresh as paint, lithe as a linnet, gay laugh, my feet bounced on the carpet, never felt better ... still have resources, still full of ambition ... you'll see, tomorrow, the next day, I'll be as spry as ever ...

JANET. The point is, he served a purpose, no doubt about that ... now, in his final moments, as darkness begins to fall ...

ALEC. Still bright as morning, I'll put myself under the severest discipline, cut out all fats and starches, cut down on cigars, rise like a lark, up pens and at 'em ...

JANET. Mmmm ... In his last moments, as the blood began to cool, Alec Kooning had, for the first time, a moment of bright clarity ...

ALEC. Yes, Janet, up pens and at 'em, the unborn words ... you'll see, you'll see, years not beyond recall, ambitions fulfilled, lights on in the old avenues of my mind, bands playing ... Janet ...

JANET. Mmmm ... tired, defeated, an old trouper ... stumbles across the stage to a storm of boos and hisses ...

ALEC. So it's no good pretending I don't exist, no good pretending I'm not a factor, a very relevant factor, no good pretending I'm not here, in full health and vigour ...

JANET. ... his voice growing hoarse ... overwhelmed with a fit of violent coughing ...

ALEC. Occasionally (Coughs) ... occasionally ... a bit ... a bit ... under the weather ... God knows ... who isn't ... a veritable juvenile is ... sometimes ... overwhelmed ... by a storm of ... coughing ... oh, God ... oh, God ...

JANET. ... puts his head in his hands ... begins to weep ...

146

(He does so)

... broken old phrases ... the last act ...

ALEC. (weeping) What gets me, what really gets me, Janet, is not merely ... the way ... you seem to have written me off ... not merely that ... though that is enough, God knows, to break the heart of a grosser, of a grosser ... spirit ... but ... on top of all that ... the way you keep on insisting, insisting ... I'm not old, I tell you ... not old at all ... spring-time of age ... an Indian summer ... I exist, I tell you, exist, in my own right, in my own ... right ...

JANET. Poor old thing ...

ALEC. I'll rise up ... majestic ...

JANET. Raises its arms ...

(He does so)

JANET. ... drops them, exhausted ... slumps down into its seat ... closes its eyes ...

ALEC. Sometimes ... your own body ... betrays you ... has a will of its own ... nothing abnormal in that ...

JANET. Poor old thing ...

ALEC. Nothing ... abnormal ... in that ...

(The light fades on JANET's side, leaving her in darkness. From now on we have a monologue for two! The point is to suggest that ALEC and JANET are somehow fused or in the relationship of character to author)

JANET. ... abnormal ...

ALEC. ... in that ... yes ... I'm not old ...

JANET. ... just tired of it ...

147

ALEC. (half a word behind, as if repeating a lesson, but reluctantly) ... just tired of it ...

JANET. ... exhausted with it ...

ALEC. ... exhausted with it ...

JANET. ... the futility of it ...

ALEC. ... the futility of it ...

JANET. ... wouldn't mind ...

ALEC. ... wouldn't mind ...

JANET. ... oblivion ...

ALEC. ... oblivion ... (Shouts) No ... Mighty Mouse will come to judge both the quick and the slow ... the cat has got me in her terrible jaws, the cat has got her teeth in my head ... Mighty Mouse, save me, patron of Orpheus, save me from this horrible, female, author ...

JANET. ... putting my hand in the drawer, Mr. Kooning,

(He does so)

for the last fearful act ... pulls out a ... Luger ...

ALEC. ... oooh ... great war stuff, took from the hand of a dead German, shells overhead ... No ... fit as a fiddle ... fit as a ...

JANET. ... last curtain ... ring of dark faces, the author hunts her character to his final disaster ...

ALEC. No ... take-over bid ... the female psyche ... it won't do ...

JANET. ... fearful the last moment, he puts a brave face on it, nothing else to be done, clicks open the revolver, bright, stinging demons, slugs go gezonk in his brain ...

148

ALEC. (his voice weaker) No ... no ...

JANET. ... darker and deeper the lights go ... takes a
last look ...

ALEC. ... No ... would've preferred strychnine or one
of the barbiturates ...

JANET. ...takes a last look, bird at the window, mouse on
the mantlepiece, keeps a straight face, remembers ...
remembers ... the safety catch ... squeezes,
squeezes, squeezes ... (The gun fires) ... the
trigger ... the end.

(ALEC slumps over his desk in a classic dead
posture, a bright pool of red gore spreads from his
hair ... The lights go up on JANET's side. She
snaps shut her book. She is, of course, MRS
ROSENBERG. She swivels round from the contempl-
ation of her dead hero ... takes pen and paper, begins
to write)

JANET. April 29th 1969 (Or whatever the date of any performance happens to be) Dear Mr. Hepplewhite,
Thank-you for your letter and your indulgent remarks
about my little piece. Originally I had intended to call
it "The Decline and Fall of a Fifth-Rate Writer" but
that seemed a bit like tempting Providence, as it
were, so I didn't. Actually, there is an element of
autobiography in it, as young man I once knew, of
slight promise, cut off in the last war, but the rest is
fiction. Yes, it does have something to do with the
will to live, the will to die, the fragmentation of the
human psycho in our modern age, the curious mixture
of farce and misery which is the slight ripple left
by the receding impulse of tragedy, something like
that, the overpowering of the male psyche, the end of
the heroic impulse, that sort of thing. No, I did not
attend the first night, couldn't summon up the courage,
all those critics, sitting like stone statues, holding
their iron pens in their hands, dipping them into my
blood. No, I couldn't manage that. You are right,
incidentally, I do admire Beckett, the voice of our age,
but I don't see an influence, nor any from Jerry,

149

E.M. Forster, Ionesco, John Osborne, Samuel Well-
born or Jean-Jacques Rousseau, to refer to only a
few of those that you mention. We all suck at the same
teat ... and, anyway, it doesn't really work like
that. Still, all I wanted to do was to say 'thank-you'
for your remarks. It is pleasant to know that one
can reach the ear of the younger generation, a sort
of defeat of time. Yours sincerely, Janet Kooning.
P.S. How clever of you by the way. Yes, there was
an alternative ending.

(ALEC opens one eye, looks interested)

In it, after many trials and tribulations, Alec and
Janet come together ...

(ALEC gets up, smiling. MRS ROSENBERG removes
her wig(?) etc. to appear as JANET. They get up,
hold hands ...)

ALEC. He wrote a best-selling novel, called "The Carpet
　　　Beaters".

JANET. She became a charming and gifted housewife,
　　　noted for her plain but beautiful cooking ...

ALEC. ... and needless to say ...

JANET ... they lived happily ever after ...

ALEC AND JANET. Isn't that nice.

(They kiss, bow to the audience, hand in hand, she
ruffles his hair, they kiss, bow again. Exit.

Red Sails in the Sunset plays, as it has done at the
opening of the play and at each break)

(Note that the dates of the letters, apart from November
11th, can be changed so as to fit the date for the
performance)

C AND B PLAYSCRIPTS

PS 44	THE SLEEPERS DEN and OVER GARDENS OUT Peter Gill	*25s	+10s0d
PS 45	THE MAROWITZ MACBETH Charles Marowitz	*25s	+9s0d
PS 46	SLEUTH Anthony Shaffer	*25s	+9s0d
* PS 47	SAMSON and ALISON MARY FAGAN David Selbourne	*25s	+9s0d
* PS 48	OPERETTA Witold Gombrowicz tr. Louis Iribarne	*25s	+9s0d

*Hardcover   +Paperback

* All plays marked thus are represented for dramatic
  presentation by
  C and B (Theatre) Ltd, 18 Brewer Street, London W1

GAMBIT

INTERNATIONAL THEATRE REVIEW

Calder and Boyars also publish a quarterly theatrical review, GAMBIT. This exciting and informative magazine was first established in order to bring new plays to a wider audience, intending to bridge the gap between the nember of good new plays being written and the number of these plays which are staged in important theatres.

Each issue contains the text of at least one full-length play as well as an editorial, articles on current trends in the theatre and coverage of new plays and productions throughout the world.

Past contributors to the magazine have included Jean-Paul Sartre, Eugene Ionesco, Jack McGowran, David Tutaev, Paolo Levi, Fernando Arrabal and Max Frisch.